Secundus Janus, Jean Bonnefons

Basia

The kisses of Joannes Secundua and Jean Bonnefons - with a selection from the

best ancient and modern authors

Secundus Janus, Jean Bonnefons

Basia
The kisses of Joannes Secundua and Jean Bonnefons - with a selection from the best ancient and modern authors

ISBN/EAN: 9783337313814

Printed in Europe, USA, Canada, Australia, Japan

Cover: Foto ©Andreas Hilbeck / pixelio.de

More available books at **www.hansebooks.com**

5497

BASIA

THE KISSES

OF

Joannes Secundus

and

JEAN BONNEFONS

With Selections

Basía:

THE KISSES

OF

JOANNES SECUNDUS

AND

JEAN BONNEFONS:

WITH

A Selection

FROM THE

BEST ANCIENT AND MODERN AUTHORS.

NEW YORK:

PUBLISHED BY CALVIN BLANCHARD,
82 Nassau Street.

1860.

CONTENTS

PREFACE.

———

AFTER the very enthusiastic eulo-·
giums bestowed upon the Kisses of
Secundus and Bonnefons, we need not
be diffident in expressing ourselves
in favor of their peculiar graceful-
ness, nor hesitate to pronounce them
as highly-polished performances.

Our Authors' Poems are all beauty,

all enchantment. The writers lead us so insensibly along with them, that we sympathise even in their excesses; yet in these beautiful Odes there is a delicacy of sentiment not to be found in any other poet. In their poetry, Secundus and Bonnefons are sportive without being wanton, and ardent without being licentious:

" They are infants of the Muses, and lisp in numbers:"

Their descriptions are warm; but the warmth is in the *ideas*, not in the *words*.

Simplicity, however, is the distinguishing characteristic of the whole of the Pieces selected for this unique volume:—they interest by their innocence, while they fascinate by their transcendent beauty.

To infer the moral disposition of a Poet from the tone of sentiment which pervades his works, is frequently a very fallacious analogy; but the souls of our Poets speak so unequivocally through their poetry, that we may consult them as the faithful mirrors of their hearts.

A few Notes have been appended with the view of saving farther reference.

There is very little known with certainty of the lives of our Poets; but some trifling information has been collected by their editors, which they found, from time to time, scattered through the writings of their contemporaries.

MEMOIR

OF

JOANNES SECUNDUS.

———

NICOLAIUS EVERARDUS, the father of
Joannes Secundus, was an excellent legal
scholar; and his learning and abilities
attracted the attention of the Emperor
Charles V. who raised him to the dignity
of President of the States of Holland
and Zealand. He was subsequently ad-
vanced to the chair of the Council of
Mechlin, which he held till his death
in 1532.

The subject of this Memoir was born
at the Hague, on the 28th of Decem-
ber, 1511, and baptized by the name of
Joannes Secundus, from his being the
second child of that name. He received
the rudiments of his education under his
paternal roof; but he was afterwards
sent to Bruges, and placed under the
care of a man of extensive erudition,
and with whom he remained until death
deprived him of that able man's instruc-
tions.

The talents of Secundus exhibited
themselves at a very early period, for
he wrote poetry in the tenth year of his
age. Painting and sculpture frequently
occupied his leisure hours; and in both
of these arts he excelled.

When our poet had attained his twen-
tieth year, his father became anxious

that he should be called to the bar; and, for that purpose, he was placed under the care of a gentleman of high repute for legal knowledge, who resided in France.

In 1533, Secundus went to Spain, where, by the influence of his friends, he became secretary to the Archbishop of Toledo. Soon after his arrival in that country, he became acquainted with Venerilla; but she had no charms for him, and he left her for the fascinating and accomplished Neæra.* To the acquaintance with this lady we are indebted for "The Kisses," a work which has so enhanced his fame as a poet. In a few months, however, the poet discovered the real character of the woman who had so captivated him; and as he began to

* See Notes on the Kisses of Secundus, p. 55

suffer from the effects of the climate, he evinced an anxiety to return to his native country.

Secundus soon found the most beneficial effects from the change of situation, and he so far recovered his health as to accept employment from the bishop of Utrecht, and then the appointment of first prothonotary to the Emperor Charles the Fifth, at that time in Italy. But death terminated his career at St. Amand, in Tournay, where he fell a victim to an inflammatory fever which carried him off in four days, on the 18th of October, 1536, in the twenty-fifth year of his age. He was interred in the monastic churchyard of St. Amand, where a marble monument, with a Latin inscription, was erected by his relations.

MEMOIR

JEAN BONNEFONS.

———

ALTHOUGH the Basia of Bonnefons will
not bear the test of comparison with those
of Secundus, yet they have been much
admired for their natural and graceful
ease, and for their warm and passionate
language.

We are unable to trace any particulars
of the family of our author. From a few
brief notices, however, which have been
collected, it appears that Bonnefons was
born at Clermont in France, in 1554,

educated for the bar, and was also of a convivial and social disposition.

The appearance of the Kisses * of Bonnefous in 1587, attracted the attention of the literary world, and many hyperbolical compliments were paid to the genius of the author. On the marriage, however, of Bonnefons, he relinquished poetry, and devoted himself to domestic affairs.

It is conjectured that our poet died in 1614, in the sixty-first year of his age.

The Poems of Bonnefons have been repeatedly printed; and the author revised an edition of his works a short time previously to his death.

The Kisses of Bonnefons were produced under the e of Pancharis, a name which the writer selected for the fair object to whom his poems were addressed.

The Kisses

OF

JOHANNES SECUNDUS.

ON HIS BOOK OF KISSES.

(Epigram, xxiv. Lib. I.)

—

Too chaste are my strains
Lycinna complains,
And despises and laughs at my kisses outright,
While, with her in league,
That soul of intrigue,
Ælia, cries that the poet is passionless quite.

But the wantons, forsooth,
Only drive at the truth,
And are dying to know what his hardship can do:
No, no, ye may long,
Neither he, nor his song,
Nor the kisses he breathes are intended for you.

The fresh blooming bride,
While she lies by his side,
Shall read her young husband a lesson from me;
And the bride, in return,
From her husband shall learn
How their joys may be varied in every degree.

THE KISSES

OF

JOHANNES SECUNDUS.

—————

KISS I.

THE ORIGIN OF THE KISS.

When in her lap the parent queen of love
Had borne Ascanius to Cythera's grove,
On a sweet couch of tender violets made,
Hush'd in repose, her precious charge she laid,
Then all around bade milk-white roses bloom,
And every air impregn'd with sweet perfume.

  Adonis' image to her mind return'd;
Once more her soul with tender passion burn'd;
And oft she cried, in ecstasy of joy,
Such was Adonis! such the lovely boy!

Oft, as in rapture o'er the youth she hung,
Her eager arms around his neck had flung,
But fear'd to break the artless sleeper's rest,
And the fond ardour of her soul repress'd;
And on each rose that blossom'd round his head
A thousand, thousand burning kisses shed.
Beneath her lips the conscious flow'rets blush'd,
O'er every bud a warmer colour rush'd;
While sighs, in gently murmur'd sounds, confess'd
Each tender wish that struggled in her breast.
Where touch her lips the bursting buds disclose
A glowing kiss in every blushing rose,
And in each fresh-blown flow'ret multiply
The thrilling transports of Dione's joy.

But when again her native realm she sought,
Drawn by her cygnets o'er the azure vault,
As through the void her chariot roll'd along,
Thrice mutt'ring, as she went, the magic song,
Like Celeus' son of old, her lavish hand
Shed kisses round, and fertiliz'd the land:
Thence for mankind the teeming harvest rose,
And hence the balm that mitigates my woes.

All hail! ye kisses of ambrosial birth,
Whom rapture's thrilling hour produc'd on earth!
Sweet joys, that sooth the pangs of fierce desire,
For you the bard shall wake the sounding lyre;

And while the muses' hill shall last, your praise
Shall live immortal in the poet's lays:
And Love! who boasts himself, with conscious
     pride,
To that dear race from which ye spring allied,
In Roman strains your raptures shall rehearse
In all the liquid melody of verse.

KISS II.

As round its neighbouring elm entwine
The amorous tendrils of the wanton vine;
    As round the oak the ivy flings,
And winds its creeping sprays, and closely clings;
    So let thy arms, Neæra, thrown
Around my neck, such fervent pressure own;
    And I as closely will entwine
My arms, and clasp that snowy neck of thine;
    And fix, in ecstasy of bliss,
On thy fair lips—one long—one never-ending kiss.
    Though Ceres pour her countless treasures
Though rosy Bacchus call to festive pleasures
    Though care-deceiving sleep invite;
For them I will not quit the dear delight;

Nor shall they tempt me to forego
   The transports that thy ruby lips bestow;
      But, fainting with the rapturous joy.
Our mingling spirits shall united fly;
   And, wafted o'er the Stygian flood,
In the same bark seek Pluto's pale abode:
      Thence reach those fields where sweet per-
         fumes
Scent every gale, and spring for ever blooms,
   And heroines of old renown'd,
And heroes with victorious laurels crown'd,
   In shady vales, and myrtle bowers,
With harmless sports beguile the fleeting hours;
   Or weave th' alternate song, or glance
Down the gay measures of the mazy dance.
      There, through the laurel's tremulous shade,
Sighs the warm breeze along the flowery glade;
   Beneath the purple violet glows,
The pale narcissus, and the blushing rose:
   Spontaneous there, the womb of earth,
Untouch'd by shares, gives teeming harvests birth.
      At our approach the happy shades
Shall rise, and welcome to those flowery glades;
   And me, with one accord, they'll place
By Homer's side among the tuneful race:
   To thee, the fairest of the fair,
Nymphs lov'd by Jove shall yield the pref'rence
      there;

Nor Helen, though of race divine,
Disdain to own inferior charms to thine.

———

KISS III.

Give me, sweet maid, one little kiss,
   One little kiss, I said, and sigh'd;
Scarce had I felt the thrilling bliss,
   Scarce were your glowing lips to mine ap-
     plied,

When from my lips your lips you take
   In sudden haste, and burst away;
So, when he feels the coiling snake,
   The heedless rustic startles in dismay.

Not this to give the balmy kiss:
   Ah! no, my love, but in the mind
To raise the fond idea of bliss,
   Then leave the sting of fierce desire behind.

KISS IV.

'Tis not a kiss those ruby lips bestow,
  But richest nectar and ambrosial dews;
Such as from fragrant nard, or cassia flow,
  Or blest Arabia's spicy shrubs diffuse:
Or sweets that from Hymettus' thymy brow,
  Or roses that Cecropian bowers produce,
Unwearied honey-bees selecting bear
To cells of virgin wax, and temper there.
  But if thy vermeil lips, in ev'ry kiss,
Thus give to banquet on celestial fare,
  And thrill my soul with ecstasy of bliss,
Soon shall this frame imbibe celestial powers,
And I shall revel in Olympian bowers.
Then spare the precious boon, Neæra, spare,
Or with me those immortal honours share!
For ev'n should Jove, by rebel godheads driven,
To me resign the majesty of heaven:
That heaven without thy presence were unblest,
And all its nectar'd feasts without a zest!

KISS V.

WHILE circled by those fond, endearing arms
  That here and there in amorous fervour twine,
Neæra, you, with soul-entrancing charms,
  Or on my neck, or shoulders soft recline,
And, fondly hanging o'er, unfold to sight
That beauteous neck, and bosom snowy white;
  And to my lips your glowing lips you join,
And on my cheek the thrilling joy indite,
Then, gently murmuring, chide your ardent swain,
If the fond jest he pay you back again.

While to my lips, in tremulous ecstasy,
  Your lips, dear maid, the thrilling kiss impart;
And, breathing forth the sweetly murmur'd sigh,
  Pour your warm spirit through my raptur'd
      heart—
That sigh to me with genial life replete,
So softly musical, so balmy sweet:
  While you, Neæra, snatch my breath away
That, glowing with my bosom's inward heat,
  Fleets on my lips, and 'most forgets to play;

And, oh! sweet soother of my passion's rage!
  Once more, with that re-animating breath,
  Recall my spirit from the gates of death,
And the fierce ardour of my soul assuage:
Impassion'd with the bliss—" With Love," I cry,
" O'er every power supreme in sovereignty—
  With Love, nor god nor mortal can compare;
But, oh! with him if any power can vie,
  'Tis you, Neæra, you, my charming fair!"

———

KISS VI.

To crown our raptures 'twas agreed, dear maid,
  A sweet two thousand should the number be;
And on thy glowing lips a thousand paid,
  A thousand kisses I received from thee:
Complete, I own, the number'd raptures prove,
But when did numbers e'er suffice with love?

When the ripe autumn yellows all the plain,
  Or spring with verdure clothes the blooming
    field,
For number'd harvests asks the anxious swain,
  Or counts the blades the grassy meadows yield;

Or importunes with prayer the god of wine,
With numoer'd leaters to enrich the vine?

Who from the guardian of the hive demands
  A thousand honey-bees, yet asks no more?
Or when the Thunderer bids his lavish hands
  On the parch'd earth refreshing waters pour,
Strive we to count each drop of falling rain
As the swift torrents moisten all the plain?

When Jove in terror clothes his angry arm,
  And hail descends, and wasting whirlwinds fly,
While earth and ocean, shook with pale alarm,
  Feel all the loosen'd vengeance of the sky,
Unmov'd he views the mischiefs they perform,
Nor measures out the horrors of the storm.

Or good or ill alike descend from heaven,
  Extremes in both adorn the race of Jove:
O thou! to whom celestial charms are given,
  Ah! why this sparing of thy bounty prove?
O goddess! thou that godhead own'st far
Who roams blue ocean in her pearly car—

Why count thy kisses, and not count my sighs?
  Why count each kiss, nor count my every tear—
Those tears, that ever streaming from my eyes,
  Adown my cheeks and breast a channel wear!

Or cease to count thy kisses, or count all
'The signs that heave—the tears that streaming fall.

Yes, count my tears.   Yet if thou cease to count,
   O cruel maid! each kiss thy lips bestow,
Then of my sorrows heed not the amount;
   But, oh! if such can mitigate my woe,
Let the unnumber'd tears these eyes have shed,
By thy unnumber'd kisses be repaid.

———

KISS VII.

A HUNDRED sweet kisses, by hundreds told o'er,
   I'll give those red lips, my dear charmer, of thine,
And thousands by thousands as lavishly pour
   On those cheeks, and those eyes that bewitch-
      ingly shine ;
Till the sums of my raptures as numberless grow
   As the drops that in ocean incessantly roll ;
Or countless as those little orbits that glow
   In the mantle of night when it covers the pole.

But, oh! when entranc'd on thy bosom I lie,
   And my lips to thy lips with fond ardour adhere ;
When I kiss thy fair cheeks or thy tale-telling eye,
   The charms that I gaz'd on at once disappear.
The sweet, pouting lips that inspir'd with delight ;
   The beam of those eyes that bewitch'd me, the
     while ;
The rose on thy cheeks are all snatch'd from my
   sight,
   And the dimple that laughs in thy delicate smile.

That delicate smile that, with solacing beam,
   Dispels from my soul all the darkness of woe,
And enlivening my bosom with hope's cheering
   gleam,
   Bids the sigh cease to heave, and the tear-drop
     to flow.
So Sol, when he rises, dispels from the sky
   The mists that would gather, and darken his way,
And borne on his gem-studded chariot on high,
   From the cloudless serene pours the splendor
     of day.

Ah me! thus, by jealous emotion possess'd,
   What rivalry glows 'twixt my lips and my eyes
Each fondly admires thee, and longs to be blest,
   And envies the pleasure the other enjoys.

Then, oh! if with jealousy eyes disagree,
    Nor my lips bear a rival in rapture, my love,
Can I bear that another should emulate me,
    And share in thy smiles, though that rival be
        Jove?

KISS VIII.

WHAT heedless wrong could urge thee thus to tear
With furious teeth my tongue, capricious fair?
Is't not enough that, sheath'd in every part,
I feel thine arrows rankling in my heart,
But that thy teeth in wantonness must wound
That tongue on which thy praises ever sound?—
That tongue, that from the morn till parting light,
Through the long day, and sad and lingering night,
Extoll'd thy beaming eyes, thy flowing hair,
Thy beauteous neck, and bosom snowy fair;
And rais'd thy fame, in tender strains, above
Those nymphs who fir'd the soul of amorous Jove,
That in those realms where rolling planets blaze,
Ev'n gods with envy heard the lavish praise.—

That tongue, that faithful tongue, that gave thy
    name
Each fond endearing term that tenderness could
    frame;
Call'd thee my life, my soul's far dearer part,
My fond delight, the idol of my heart;
My bloom ing Venus, and my gentle love,
My beauteous turtle, and my little dove;
Till e'en the queen of charms with envy heard
Each tender epithet, each endearing word.

And does it then delight thee thus to tear
With wanton wounds my tongue, imperious fair;
Because, unmov'd by each capricious wrong,
Thy charms still form the burden of its song;
Because thy lips, and beaming eyes it sings,
And e'en those teeth from which its anguish
    springs;
Because, despite of all thy cruelty,
E'en while it bleeds, it bleeds, and lisps of thee!

O beauty, beauty! such thy powerful sway,
At once we feel thee, and at once obey!

KISS IX.

Oh! cease the balmy kiss, and cease awhile
The murmur'd rapture, the endearing smile;
Nor always thus your arms around me twine,
And faint, and breathless on my neck recline:
E'en pleasure has its bounds; the rapturous joy,
Repeated oft, will lose its zest, and cloy.
When thrice three kisses from thy lips I sue,
Withhold the seven, and give me only two;
Nor these with too much rapture be replete,
Nor yet too long, nor yet too balmy sweet;
Such as chaste Dian' to her brother gives,
Or from some artless maid her sire receives:
Then bursting from my arms, with bounding feet
Fly swift, and hide you in some dark retreat:
Close I'll pursue through each perplexing shade,
Search every spot, and find where you are laid,
And, as the towering falcon bears away
The timid dove, I'll seize my beauteous prey.
Around me then your suppliant arms you'll fling,
And hang upon my neck, and closely cling,
And on my lips seven coaxing kisses press,
And with endearments sue for your release,

But sue in vain: not seven shall set you free,
But seven times seven the price of freedom be:
Still shall my glowing arms your neck infold,
And captive still my beauteous wanton hold.
Then, when you pay the balmy ransom, swear
By all your graces, all your charms, my fair,
That oft again such frolics you'll pursue,
And oft for faults like these such balmy sums be
 due.

    —————

KISS X.

Nor certain kisses please my changeful mind,
Each has its varied rapture undefin'd;
So, when thy humid'lips encounter mine,
Sweet is the humid kiss which flows from thine;
So ardent kisses ardent joys impart,
And the warm transport thrills within the heart;
So when thine eyes with tender passion glow,
'Tis sweet to kiss the authors of my woe;
'Tis sweet to kiss thy cheeks, and breathless die
On thy fair neck with rapturous ecstasy.

    C 2

And on thy rosy cheeks the joy indite,
Thy shoulders fair, and bosom snowy white:
And while our glowing lips, in amorous play,
In rapture meet, and snatch the kiss away,
'Tis bliss to feel, as lips with lips unite,
Our souls commingling in the dear delight—
The heart forsaking with the flecting breath—
While love lies panting on the brink of death.

To me, or whether to thy lips I give,
Or from thy ruby lips the kiss receive,
Or the long kiss, when lips to lips adhere,
The soft, the rapid—all alike are dear.
Only be thine, with sweet ingenious art,
Each kiss to vary that thy lips impart ;
Nor what thy lips receive on mine bestow,
So shall our joys with varied transports flow:
But let the first who from this 'pact shall swerve,
With meek submissive looks this law observe :

   " As many kisses each at first may give,
As many kisses each at first receive,
So many kisses shall the vanquish'd pay,
So many kisses varied every way."

KISS XI.

Too warm thy kisses, youths and maidens cry,
  Too warmly told, with too much rapture fraught,
  Kisses to rugged sires of old untaught:
Hence when, while circled by my arms you lie,
And on your glowing lips entranc'd I die,
  I fain would ask what rigid censors say,
  The rapture steals me from myself away,
And thought and sense, alike bewilder'd fly.
Neæra smil'd, and, snatching to her breast,
  Around my neck eutwin'd her snowy arms,
And on my lips a sweeter kiss impress'd
    Than Mars e'er ravish'd from the queen of
      charms;
Censors like these then fears my bard? she cried;
At my tribuna must thy cause be tried.

KISS XII.

Ye blooming maids; ye modest matrons, say
  Why from my pages thus avert your eyes?
  Nor there, distain'd with foul indecencies,
The furtive jokes that amorous godheads play
Ye read, for pure, and simple is my lay;
  Such as even pedagogues, with looks austere,
  May read, and beardless striplings safely hear:
Yet maids and matrons turn their eyes away
When I, chaste votary of the tuneful nine,
  Sing the chaste kiss, and blush with deep offence
Because, forsooth, few glowing phrases shine:
  Hence, squeamish maids! fastidious matrons
    hence!
Neæra, chaster far than you, approves
As well th' offenceless verse, but the warm poe
    loves.

KISS XIII.

Faint with the rapturous joy, and breathless
        grown,
Around thy neck my languid arms were thrown,
And on my burning lips, prepar'd to part,
Hover'd my soul, and ceas'd to warm my heart;
Pale Styx already swam before my sight,
And hell's grim pilot, and the shades of night,
When, gently breathing from thy inmost breast,
Thy lips on mine a humid kiss impress'd:
That kiss redeem'd me from the Stygian vale,
And bade th' infernal vessel freightless sail.
But, ah! no freightless voyage th' pilot made,
Still in those regions flits my plaintive shade;
Breath'd in this frame, a part of thee remains,
Part of thy soul, and these faint limbs sustains;
But through each passage, eager to be free,
It pants, it struggles to revert to thee;
And, oh! unless thy fostering breath retain,
Life will desert this sinking frame again.
Then to my lips thy lips, Neæra, join,
And with thy soul sustain this soul of mine!

So, when this scene of life and love is o'er,
From our joint frames one single soul shall soar.

———

KISS XIV.

Way tempt me with those lips of scarlet glow?
  For learn, O maiden, with the flinty breast,
  Ne'er shall those proffer'd lips by mine be
    press'd!
Since you would have me prize your kisses so,
Those cold, cold kisses whence no raptures flow,
  That when, all glowing with the wild desire,
  In every pulse I feel the scorching fire,
As the warm life-blood rushes to and fro,
You thus refuse me, and my pangs deride.
  But whither now? oh! fly me not, but stay;
Oh! turn not, turn not those sweet lips aside;
  Oh! turn not thus those sparkling eyes away;
Yes! I will kiss thee, to thy lips be press'd,
Dear maid, more gentle far than cygnet's downy
    breast!

KISS XV.

'GAINST thee, my life, he stood prepar'd to wing
The fiery shaft, and stretch'd the sounding string;
But when thy blooming cheeks, thy forehead fair
The wanton ringlets of thy flowing hair,
And those thy gently heaving breasts he spied,
Those breasts that with his beauteous mother's
    vied,
Love paus'd in doubt, enamour'd of thy charms.
Then flung the dart aside, and sought thy arms:
There on thy lips with childish transport hung,
And kiss'd and wanton'd as he fondly clung—
Breath'd Cyprian odours in each kiss he press'd,
And fill'd with fragrant sweets thy inmost breast
Then by each god the solemn oath he swore,
And lovely Venus, ne'er to harm thee more.
What wonder then such sweets thy kiss imbue,
Such balmy fragrance, such ambrosial dew!
What wonder then thy heart can never prove,
Oh, cruel maid! the gentle fires of love.

KISS XVI.

On ' brighter than that planet far
 That sheds her silvery beams at eve,
Fairer than Venus' golden star
 Sweet maid, a hundred balmy kisses give;
As many as th' impassion'd bard could crave,
As many as his beauteous Lesbia gave;

 As countless as the charms that play
  Around those lips with crimson dyed;
 As countless as the loves that stray
  O'er those fair cheeks, and in their blushes
   hide;
As countless as the lives your eyes impart;
As countless as the deaths your glances dart:

 As countless as the hopes and fears,
  As countless as the lover's sighs;
 As countless as the ceaseless cares
  That ever mingle with his tenderest joys;
Or as those arrows sheath'd within my breast,
Or those that still in love's bright quiver rest.

But mingle all your balmy kisses
    With fond endearments, mirth, and smiles;
With soft delights, with murmuring blisses,
    With love-inspiring jests, and wanton wiles:
So, in returning spring, the billing doves
With quivering pinions interchange their loves.

And while upon my cheek you lie,
    Your senses lost in amorous trance,
And here and there, in rapturous joy,
    Your passion-beaming eyes voluptuous glance,
To me in sweetly plaintive murmurs sigh,
" Support me, dearest, for I faint, I die!"

My circling arms around you throwing,
    I'll press you to my beating heart;
And the long, humid kiss bestowing,
    Recall the fleeting sense, and life impart:
Till, with the frequent rapture breathless grown,
In dewy kisses I expire my own.

And cry, in accents faint and low,
    " In those dear arms, my love, uphold me!"
Then round me your fond arms you'll throw,
    And closely to your fost'ring bosom fold me;
And pressing on my lips the glowing kiss,
Call back my fainting soul to life, and bliss.

Thus, lovely maid, while yet we may,
  Improve the moments as they fly,
While life is in its vernal day,
  And youth invites us with a smiling eye:
Soon with its cares will frowning age be here,
And pale disease, and death close pressing on his
    rear.

———

KISS XVII.

A BRIGHTER crimson, with the morning light,
  Blushes the rose impearl'd with nightly dew
  So glow thy ruby lips with brighter hue,
Moist with the kisses of a rapturous night;
  And thy fair cheeks a fairer tint assume
From violets, as some hand of lily white;
    So new ripe cherries shine 'midst lingering
      bloom,
When spring, and summer in the tree unite.
    But, ah! when thus thy kisses sweetest flow,
Why forc'd to leave thee, and forego their
      charms!
    Still let thy lips retain that beauteous glow
Till eve restores me to thy circling arms!

Yet if some happier rival there be blest,
Pale may they turn as mine by jealous fears
	possess'd!

KISS XVIII.

ON A BUST OF HIS MISTRESS IN WAX.

The moulded wax when Venus chanc'd to view,
Where shone thy ruby lips with brighter hue,
As the red coral mix'd with ivory glows,
And 'midst the circling white a deeper colour
	shows;
With envy fir'd, a flood of tears she shed,
And call'd her loves around, and sobbing said:

  "Ah! what avails me now, on flowery Ide
T' have conquer'd Pallas, and Jove's sister bride
When to these purple lips, with partial eyes,
The Phrygian shepherd 'judg'd the golden prize,
If ever thus, extoll'd with lavish praise,
The fair transcends me in the poet's lays!
Go then, ye little loves, and on his head
Avenge the wrong, and all your fury shed;

Lodge deep your venom'd shafts in every part,
And empty all your quivers in his heart;
But touch not with your glowing fires the maid,
For her reserve your chilling shafts of lead;
Cold and insensate must her heart remain,
And the warm current freeze in every vein."

   She said: and now through all my melting soul
The fiery torments rage without control;
While you, with icy heart, in cruel scorn,
Laugh at the tortures by your lover borne,
Cold and insensate as the rock that braves
Sicilia's seas, or Adria's dashing waves.
For you I suffer, too ungrateful fair,
Your ruby lips provok'd the ills I bear;
But you, alas! with causeless hate pursue,
Nor care what love, and angry gods can do!
Yet cease, oh, lovely maid! the cruel scorn,
That ill becomes the face such charms adorn;
And let those lips, the cause of all my woes—
Those ruby lips where balmy nectar flows—
Oh! let those honied lips to mine be press'd,
And drink the poison from my inmost breast,
Till through your frame the warm infection steals,
And all your soul the mutual ardour feels:
Nor fear the gods, nor dread the queen of love,
Beauty like yours should sway the powers above.

KISS XIX

WHY search for sweets in every flow'ret's bloom
The thyme, the anise, scatt'ring sweet perfume;
The blushing rose, the violet's nectar'd flower,
Ambrosial offspring of the vernal hour?
Fly, silly insects, to my charming fair,
Light on her lips, and gather fragrance there—
Lips where the thyme, and blushing rose dispense
Their rich perfumes, and ravish every sense;
Where vernal violets all their sweets exhale,
And fragrant anise breathes in every gale—
Lips by Narcissus' genuine tears bedew'd—
Lips by th' Œbalian stripling's blood imbued;
Pure as those streams where either ceas'd to be,
He by foul chance, and self-enamour'd he
That fragrant life-blood, and those flowing tears,
By nectar temper'd, and ethereal airs,
Whose balmy tides impregn'd the fruitful earth,
And gave the vari-colour'd flow'rets birth.

  Permit me too, ye happy bees, to share
The honied treasures that ye gather there;

Nor thence, rapacious, ravish all their store
Till your o'er-loaded cells can beer no more,
Lest, when again my burning lips I press,
No sweets refresh me, and no raptures bless;
And I, in madd'ning disappointment, mourn
A babbler's meed, my folly's just return.

But, oh! sweet insects, while ye revel there,
Nor point your stings, nor wound the beauteous
    fair:
Weapons as keen her glances dart around,
Nor unaveng'd shall pass the wanton wound,
Gently, oh! gently, happy insects, sip
The balmy fragrance of her honied lip.

EPITHALAMIUM.

HAIL, genial hour!
In myrtle bow'r
Of young-eyed Pleasure born;
  Whom wanton wiles,
  And jests, and smiles,
And roseate sports adorn.

  Sweet hour, all hail!
  With envy pale,
Which Jove himself might see;
  And own at least
  The nectar'd feast
Equall'd, sweet hour! by thee.

  No happier hour
  The Gnydian power
Could on blest man bestow;
  Nor he, who reigns
  O'er farthest plains,
God of the fatal bow.

D

Young Cupid, wild
As any child,
Who shakes his purple wings;
And some rich joy,
Delicious boy!
On every sorrow flings;

Nor thou, great Queen,
Unrivall'd seen,
With wondrous grace to move;
At Love's high feast
A bidden guest,
Sister and wife of Jove.

Nor, Hymen, thou,
Upon the brow
Of tuneful mountain born;
Who dwell'st in bowers
Of am'rous flowers,
And, from her mother torn,

Lead'st much afraid,
Much pleas'd, the maid,
(Midst doubts, and hopes, and sighs,)
To the dear youth,
Who, full of truth,
In wild expectance lies.

O hour of bliss,
To equal this
Olympus strives in vain;
O happy pair,
O happy fair,
O happy, happy swain!

Hail, wedded boy,
Whose only joy
Soon in thy arms shall rest
And face to face,
In fond embrace
Sink gently on thy breast.

She, who all day
An infant lay
Prattling at Beauty's feet;
Who kiss'd the child,
And, as it smil'd,
Breath'd o'er it every sweet;

Breath'd charms so bright,
That at the sight
Venus shrank back with awe:
And from her skies,
With envious eyes,
Indignant Juno saw

A nobler mien:
E'en Wisdom's queen
With female anger glow'd;
And ask'd what chance,
At each proud glance,
Such matchless gifts bestow'd?

Should they all three
Once more agree
To visit Ida's shade;
And should again
The shepherd swain
Be of the contest made

Sole judge; no more
To Paphos' bow'r
Would laughing Venus bear
The prize away;
No longer say,
" I'm fairest of the fair "

But with one choice,
With one loud voice,
Hers would the apple be
In features, sense,
And elegance,
Who most resembled thee.

EPITHALAMIUM.

O hour of bliss,
To equal this
Olympus strives in vain;
O happy pair,
O happy fair,
O happy, happy swain!

Hail, happy bride,
Thy husband's pride,
soon, in eager fold,
The conscious bed,
With blushes red,
virgin neck shall hold.

Long hath the fire
Of slow desire
early prime consum'd,
Marking, as blows
The op'ning rose,
thy young beauties bloom'd.

Thy breast of snow,
Thy lips that glow
calth divinely warm;
And thy bright hair,
With artless care
ose wanton ringlets charm

EPITHALAMIUM.

　　' Ne'er will the sun
　　' His circuit run ;'
Impatient of delay,
　　He sighing cries:
　　' O moon, arise!
' O come, O come away!

　　' Come, mildly bright,
　　' Pure orb of light,
' To thee such scenes belong :
　　' Come, every star,
　　' And from afar
' Begin the bridal song.'

　　O hour of bliss,
　　To equal this
Olympus strives in vain ,
　　O happy pair,
　　O happy fair,
O happy, happy swain !

　　Cease, cease thy fears,
　　Thy vows, and tears,
O, fervent bridegroom, cease ;
　　Soon shall thy heart,
　　No more to part,
Resume its long-lost peace.

EPITHALAMIUM.

Soon from her throne
Of cygnets' down,
With many a chaplet gay,
Love's constant friend,
Shall Venus bend,
And chide the ling'ring day.

She chides;—and see
The burning sea
Its radiant god receives;
Faintly he gleams,
And his shorn beams
In blushing billows laves.

See in her hand
An ebon wand,
How his lov'd sister guides
Her silver car,
Sweet wanderer,
Climbing heaven's crystal sines.

Mark too that star,
To virgins dear,
Hesper! with glitt'ring head
Who loves his train
O'er the blue train
In golden ranks to lead.

O hour of bliss,
To equal this
Olympus strives in vain;
O happy pair,
O happy fair,
O happy, happy swain!

Now shall the maid
At length be laid,
A rich, unspotted prize;
Now youth, beware,
Be thine the care,
That she no maid arise.

Now, plac'd in bed,
With unfeign'd red
Her beauteous face shall glow;
Now shall she fear
Thy tread to hear,
And hope, and wish it now.

Perhaps a tear,
As crystal clear,
In trickling haste may flow;
Perhaps with sighs
Your heart she tries,
Or murm'ring vents her woe.

But mind not thou
The tears that flow
Mind not the piteous sigh;
Soft soothing speak,
And her wet cheek
Wipe with thy kisses dry.

O hour of bliss,
To equal this
Olympus strives in vain;
O happy pair,
O happy fair,
O happy, happy swain'

Thus when supine,
With lips divine
She prints the nuptial bed·
And, like a flow'r
With hasty show'r
O'ercome, her virgin head

Hangs down in shame
When o'er her frame
Soft languors gently creep
And the clos'd eye,
Unknowing why,
Attempts in vain to sleep;

EPITHALAMIUM.

When at the side
Of thy dear bride
Thou liest, Dione's care;
Happier in love
Than am'rous Jove,
Than monarchs happier far

Then, in full tides
Whilst vigour glides,
Trembling through ev'ry vein.
Begin the fight
Of fierce delight,
Of pleasure mix'd with pain.

Then, let the kiss
Of humid bliss
O'er her sweet body fly;
O'er her warm check,
Her eyes, her neck,
And lips of luscious dye.

Oft shall she cry,
'O cruel, he!'
Oft weeping say, 'Forbear·
Oft shall her hand
Your lips withstand,
Oft meet you, you know where.

O night of bliss,
To equal this
Olympus strives in vain;
O happy pair,
O happy fair,
O happy, happy swain!

Much in defence
Of innocence,
Of virtue's nicest laws,
Will the dear maid
Affrighted plead,
And urge a moment's pause.

In vain she strives;
Enjoyment lives
On such endear'd delays;
And the wild fire
Of fierce desire,
Oppos'd, the wilder plays.

Hence, proud in arms,
O'er her rich charms
With nimblest strength you move;
Hence, bolder grown,
To the great throne
Of love insatiate rove.

EPITHALAMIUM.

What vast **excess**
Of happiness,
In show'rs of kisses **veil'd;**
When her soft cries
In softer sighs
You drown, and win the field.

O night of bliss,
To equal this
Olympus strives in vain;
O happy pair,
O happy fair,
O happy, happy swain!

Not but he'll speak
In accents meek,
Pleading his tale of love;
Soft, as when plays
The silken breeze,
That wakes the whisp'ring grove.

Soft, as when coos
The dove that woos
His mate in vernal bow'rs;
Or with sweet throat,
When her last note
The swan expiring pours:

Till vanquish'd quite
In the fond fight,
O'ercome by Cupid's dart,
    She lends her ear
    In blushing fear,
And yields her virgin heart:

Till that she lies
All bare, and cries,
' Sweet lovely murd'rer, come;'
    Expands her arms,
    Unfolds her charms,
And panting waits her doom.

O night of bliss,
To equal this
Olympus strives in vain;
    O happy pair,
    O happy fair,
O happy, happy swain!

Then shall thy lip,
Delighted, sip
The dew of nectar'd bliss:
    Then shall thy soul,
    Without control,
Enjoy the ling'ring kiss.

EPITHALAMIUM.

Then **thy** rich smiles,
And wanton wiles,
As wanton **she'll** return;
With raptures sweet,
Thy raptures meet,
And, as thou burnest, burn.

Then close to **thine**
Her mouth shall **join,**
Sucking **voluptuous death;**
Till, in one sigh
Of **ecstasy,**
Both **touch the** verge of death:

Till that, more gay
In am'rous play,
The genial **couch she shakes:**
Warm livelier **sports**
Inventive courts,
And what she wishes speaks.

O night of bliss,
To equal this
Olympus **strives in vain;**
O happy **pair,**
O happy **fair,**
O happy, **happy** swain'

Then, then, 'To arms!'
The queen of charms;
To arms!' young Cupid cries:
They hear, obey,
And urge the fray
Of sweet contentious joys.

She pants, she bleeds;
The youth succeeds;
More close they now engage:
While here and there
Love's nimble spear,
Quick-darting, fires their rage.

That wondrous spear,
Great god of war!
Which not thy sister guides:
But one more dear,
Thy mistress fair,
Who at these sports presides

Who, in such fights
Well pleas'd, delights
The rending wounds to spy
Who loves to see
Coy Chastity
A bleeding victim lie.

EPITHALAMIUM.

Mark, with what heat
They struggling meet,
How every limb's employ'd;
Till at the last,
Consuming fast,
Enjoying, and enjoy'd,

They gasp for breath
A moment's death
Th' enervate body knows;
While on each side
Love's various tide
In streams of pleasure flows.

O sight of bliss,
To equal this
Olympus strives in vain;
O happy pair,
O happy fair,
O happy, happy swain'

Rest, take your ease:
May sports like these,
With many a conscious moon,
Be oft renew'd;
As oft be view'd
By many a blushing sun!

EPITHALAMIUM.

And, oh! bless'd pair!
May offsprings dear
Soon crown your fond embrace;
Soon may there rise,
To glad your eyes,
A long and beauteous race!

Whose converse gay
Will chase away
Each heart-consuming care;
Whose infant smile
Those pains beguile,
Those pains you're doom'd to bear.

And, when old age
Life's whitest page
Shall from your sight remove,
Who on your bier
Will drop a tear—
The tear of filial love:

Rest, take your ease;
For sports like these
New strength, new ardour gain.
Rest, happy pair,
Rest, happy fair,
Rest, happy, happy swain'

E

THE REPULSE.

—

One kiss you earnestly implore,
   And I for this, dear youth, must fly thee;
That boon obtain'd, you'd ask for more,
   And I, alas! could not deny thee.

   Short would be love's tender tie,
   That strives to bind thy heart in vain;
   But then the hapless maid might sigh
   While thou wouldst triumph in her pain.

THE AUTHOR'S APOLOGY

FOR THE VOLUPTUOUSNESS OF HIS WRITINGS.

WOULD then some meddling fool inquire
   Why themes like these the poet sings,
Why soft, voluptuous thoughts inspire,
   And passion trembles in his strings?
Tell him, because I hate the race
   Of critics, and defy their rage:
It is because their dull grimace
   Shall ne'er defile my tender page.

Were kings my theme, and did I paint
   The pageant of some tyrant's state;
Or of some bigot, deem'd a saint,
   The fabled miracles relate;
Comment, and gloss, and note would spread
   Confusion o'er each tortur'd verse;
And the poor stripling while he read
   Would sigh, and deem his task a curse.

E 2

While I delight in themes like these
  That bid the soul with passion melt,
My verse shall never cease to please,
  For by the glowing heart 'tis felt:
In my soft strains the youth shall plead
  His passion to the maid ador'd;
And the warm girl, but newly wed,
  Repeat them to her youthful lord.

NOTES

KISSES OF SECUNDUS.

—

KISS I

(The subject of this poem is from Virgil.)

" Had borne Ascanius to Cythera's grove."

Ascanius (son of Æneas, and grandson of Venus)
was ..... from the flames of Troy by his father,
whom he succeeded in the kingdom of Latinus.
Cythera, (in compass about six miles,) an island
in Peloponnesus, was particularly sacred to the
goddess Venus, who rose, it is supposed by
Hesiod, the poet, from the sea near its coasts.
At Cythera, the Phœnicians dedicated a beautiful
temple to Venus.

Peloponnesus comprehends the most southern parts of
Greece. Its present .... is the Morea.
The city of Troy has been celebrated by the poems of
Homer and Virgil. The Trojan war was undertaken by

the Greeks to recover Helen, (the most beautiful woman of her time,) whom Paris, the son of Priam, the king of Troy, had carried away from the house of Menelaus, king of Sparta.

"Adonis' image to her mind return'd."

Adonis was the favourite of Venus. He was fond of hunting, and was cautioned by his mistress not to hunt wild beasts. The advice, however, he slighted; and, at last, he received a mortal bite from a wild boar, which he had wounded. Venus, after shedding many tears at his death, changed him into the flower called Anemony. Adonis was also an Assyrian idol.

"The thrilling transports of Dione's joy."

According to Homer and others, Dione was mother of Venus, by Jupiter; but Venus herself is sometimes called Dione.

"Like Celeus' son of old."

Celeus, king of Eleusis, (a town of Attica,) gave a kind reception to Ceres, (the goddess of harvests,) who in return taught his son, Triptolemus, the cultivation of the earth.

"And while the Muses' hill shall last."

Helicon, a hill of Bœtia, (a country of Greece,) was sacred to the Muses, who had there a temple.

The fountain, Hippocrene, (which first rose from the ground when struck by the horse Pegasus,) and Mount Parnassus, were also both sacred to the Muses. Parnassus is one of the highest mountains of Europe.

Hippocrene is derived from "ιππου crene," the horse's fountain.

KISS II.

(This description of Elysium is an imitation of Tibullus.)

" So let thy arms, Neæra."

Neæra was the mistress of Johannes Secundus, and to his acquaintance with this lady we are indebted for this portion of his works. The lady possessed an accomplished mind, as well as a beautiful person, and was an ardent admirer of poetry. We cannot, however, undertake to say whether his Basia are to be considered as proofs that he was passionately fond of her person, or merely as poetical compliments addressed to a woman who played with his feelings, and kept them perpetually inflamed. But a twelvemonth had scarcely passed before he discovered her

real character, when he forwarded the following
Epigram to her, which, perhaps, is a master-piece
in that style of writing:

> Thy beauty won me, and thy beaming eyes,
> Thy manners, proud Neæra, I despise,
> Naked thou pleasest not: I love thee best
> in modest garb, and unassuming vest:
> Thy glowing kisses thrill me with delight;
> Yet I do not ask thee: rash is the right.
> Nature that gave thee beauties gave beside
> A thousand faults those beauties cannot hide;
> And yet, despite of all thy faults, I feel
> Those charms resistless, and I love thee still.

> When beauty smiles, sure love has eyes can trace
> The charms that please, and number every grace;
> Not his so well who on Juno chose her sky,
> Or Lyncius famed for his discerning eye:
> Not Thamyras so keen when faults appear,
> Nor he of old renown, the Grecian seer.

There was also a Roman courtezan of the name
of Neæra, who was mistress to Tibullus, as well
as a favourite of Horace. These celebrated poets
had a poetical contest for the favours of that celebrated woman. The following is a translation of
Ode 15, Book 5, wherein Horace complains of
Neæra's breach of faith:

> It was night, when the moon shone in a serene sky
> among the lesser stars, when you, about to brave the
> divinity of the great gods, swore to be true to my re-
> quests, embracing me with your pliant arms more closely
> than the lofty oak is clasped by the ivy; that while the

wolf should remain an enemy to the flock, and Orion, opposite to the stars, should trouble the wintry sea, and would be glad of what he might get with his hands; so long as something of this sort should remain. O Nerra, you shall in no way reproach your graces with any merit. I give myself up to you greatly. Hence, he will not run into anger as a lover to the one of these nature, if someone, with anger, being provoked, he will ask for a nashy one who will return his love; and, though my anger gives sorry a should take possession of you in yet my sadness sul I not give way to that beauty which has once given me disgust.

" Though Ceres pour her countless treasures."

Ceres, the goddess of corn and harvests. She had a daughter by Jupiter, whom she called Proserpine. This daughter was carried away by Pluto, as she was gathering flowers. Ceres sought Proserpine all over Sicily; and when night came she lighted two torches at the flames of Mount Etna, to continue her search all over the world. At length Arethusa informed her that her daughter had been carried away by Pluto. Ceres immediately flew into heaven with her chariot drawn by two dragons, and demanded of Jupiter the restoration of her daughter, which the god agreed to grant, provided Proserpine had not eaten any thing in the kingdom of Pluto; but Proserpine had eat a of the grains of a pomegranate, which she had gathered as she walked over the Elysian fields: her return, therefore, was impracticable.   During the inquiries of Ceres for her daughter, the cultivation of the earth was neglected.

Jupiter was the most powerful of all the gods of the ancients   As the wife of Pluto, Proserpine became queen of hell   a Prince of Arcadia fell in love with Arethusa; but she, to avoid his courtship, fled into Sicily, where she was changed into a fountain, and her lover into a river. It was said by the ancients, that any thing thrown into the river of Alpheus, will show itself on the waters of Arethusa.—The Elysian fields were supposed by some to be in the Fortunate Islands, on the coast of Africa; on the authority of Virgil, (the poet,) they were situate in Italy; according to Lucian, they were near the moon; and in the centre of the earth, if we believe Plutarch, (the biographer.)

" Though rosy Bacchus call."

Bacchus is the Osiris (the great deity) of the Egyptians.   He was the god of vintage, of wine, and of drinkers, and is generally represented as an effeminate young man, crowned with vine and ivy leaves: sometimes, however, he appears as an infant; and at others, as an old man.   His amours were not numerous.

" And wafted o'er the Stygian flood."

Styx, a celebrated river of hell, round which it flows nine times.   The water is so cold and venomous that it is fatal to any one who drinks it.

KISS IV.

" Or, sweets that from Hymettus' thymy brow."

Hymettus is a mountain of Attica, (22 miles from Athens,) famous for its bees and excellent honey. Cecropia was the original name of Athens.

" I shall revel in Olympian bowers."

Mount Olympus was supposed by the ansients to touch the heavens; and from that circumstance, they have made it the residence of the gods and the court of Jupiter. It is, however, about a mile and a half in perpendicular height, and is covered with pleasant woods, caverns, and grottos. According to the poets, there was neither wind, rain, nor clouds, but one eternal spring on the top of this mountain.

KISS VII.

" So Sol, when he rises, dispels from the sky."

Sol (the sun) was an object of veneration among the ancients. However, Apollo, Phœbus, and Sol, are supposed to be the same divinity by some writers, though denied by others

KISS VIII.

" My blooming Venus, and my gentle dove."

Venus is the goddess of love, beauty, and mirth, when taken in the best sense ; but she is as often viewed as the patroness of lewdness, adultery, &c. Cicero mentions four of this name, which are confounded by the poets. Of these, however, the most celebrated is the Venus who sprang from the sea, and who soon after was carried to heaven, where she was admired for her beauty. Jupiter attempted to gain her affections ; but Venus refused him, when he gave her in marriage to his deformed son, Vulcan. Her intrigue with Mars is the most celebrated. The power of Venus over the heart was supported and assisted by a girdle, which gave beauty, grace, and elegance, when worn by even the most deformed. She is generally represented with her son Cupid either on a chariot drawn by doves, or by swans or sparrows.

Horace, in Ode 26, Book 3, bids farewell to Love. The following are extracts from the translation by Smart :

I lately lived a proper person *for the service of the girls,* and campaigned it not without honour.

So also in Ode 1, Book 1 :

I am not the man I was under the dominion of good

natured Cynara, (one of Horace's favourites.) For her
O...........desires to ....
Eft...........harrowed for y.........
whither ....
me, no........
mourn........
my temples with fresh flowers, delight me any longer. Yet
still in my dreams I catch thee in my arms.

KISS IX.

" Such as chaste Dian' to her brother gives."

Acco.ding to Cicero, there were three goddesses
of the name of Diana; but the daughter of Jupiter
was the most celebrated. She, out of love to
chastity, retired into the woods, and there exercised herself with her nymphs) in hunting wild
beasts. She, however, forgot her dignity to enjoy
the company of Endymion, a shepherd, whom she
cast into a deep sleep on Mount Latinus, where
he lay naked, and was so struck with his beauty,
that she afterwards came down from heaven every
night to enjoy his company. She was called in
heaven by the name of Phœbe, and was supposed
to be the same as the moon. The most famous

of her temples was that of Ephesus, which was one
of the seven wonders of the world.

According to Horace, she was protectress of the mountains, and the groves, and " attended the young women
in labour, and preserved them from death.

——

KISS XI.

" Than Mars e'er ravish'd from the queen of
charms."

According to Homer, Mars was the son of
Jupiter and Juno; but Ovid makes him the son
of Juno without a father, as Juno was anxious to
become a mother without the assistance of the
other sex. Mars was the god of war, and he
gained the affection of Venus, and gratified his
desires. Vulcan was informed of his wife's de-
baucheries, and he secretly placed a net around
the bed, and the two lovers were exposed in each
other's arms to the ridicule of the gods. Mars
presided over gladiators, and was the god of
hunting, and all manly exercises and amusements.

KISS XV

" Breath'd Cyprian odours in each kiss he press'd."

The term Cyprian is derived from Cyprus, a large island between Cilicia and Syria, sacred to Venus, who had many temples there, especially one at Paphos, where the virgins were permitted by the laws to obtain a dowry by prostitution.

KISS XVI.

" As many as his beauteous Lesbia gave."

The women of Lesbos were celebrated for their beauty, and for their skill in music; but the people were so dissipated, that the epithet " Lesbian" was frequently used to signify extravagance. Alcæus and Sappho, however, were natives of this place, and distinguished themselves by their poetical compositions. Lesbos (now Metelin) is a large island in the Ægean sea, and the wine there produced was as much esteemed by the ancients as by the moderns.

KISS XVIII.

(Secundus was in the habit of moulding in wax; and therefore it is presumed that he took a likeness of Neæra.)

. . . . "On flow'ry Ide
T' have conquer'd Pallas, and Jove's sister bride."

"The Phrygian shepherd 'judg'd the golden prize."

Ide (*Ida*) is a mountain in Phrygia, a small distance from Troy. It was on this mount that the shepherd Paris adjudged the prize of beauty (the golden apple) to Venus, against Juno and Minerva (Pallas.) The top of Ida was covered with green wood, and its elevation afforded a fine and extensive view of the Hellespont and the adjacent countries. Minerva received the name of Pallas because she killed the giant of that name. She is the goddess of wisdom, war, and all the liberal arts; and was the first who built a ship. Juno was sister to Jupiter, who (not insensible to her charms) more effectually to gain her confidence, changed himself into a cuckoo, raised a great storm, and rendered the air chill and cold. Under that form he went to Juno, who pitied the cuckoo and took it to her bosom. As soon as Jupiter had gained these advantages, he resumed his original

form, after he had made a solemn promise of mar
riage to his sister, he gratified his desires. By
this marriage Juno became the queen of all the
gods, and mistress of heaven and earth.

" Sicilia's seas, or Adria's dashing waves."

The whirlpool of Charybdis, on the coast of
Sicily, was very dangerous to sailors, and it proved
fatal to a part of the fleet of Ulysses. It appears
to be an agitated water from seventy to ninety
fathoms deep, circling in quick eddies. A seventy
four gun-ship has been whirled round on its
surface. On the opposite shore (Italy) there is a
dangerous rock called Scylla.

The sea of Adria is now called the gulf of Venice

KISS XIX.

" Ambrosial offspring of the vernal hour."

The food of the gods was called ambrosia, and
their drink nectar. The word ambrosia signifies
immortal, and the food, which was sweeter than
honey, and of a most odoriferous smell, had the
power to give immortality to all those who par
took of it. Juno perfumed her hair with ambrosia
when she adorned herself to captivate Jupiter.

F

' Lips by Narcissus' genuine tears bedew'd."

Narcissus was a beautiful youth, who slighted
the courtship of several nymphs; and, at last,
died for the love of himself, he having seen his
image reflected in a fountain. His blood was
changed into a flower, which still bears his name.

" Lips by th' Œbalian stripling's blood imbued."

Œbalia is the ancient name for Laconia, a
country on the southern parts of Peloponnesus.
It received its name from king Œbalus, and thence
Œbalides puer is applied to Hyacinthus, and
Œbalus sanguis is used to denominate his blood.
Hyacinthus was a beautiful boy; and when he and
Apollo were playing at quoits, Zephyrus, (from
jealousy of the boy,) with a strong blast, carried
back a quoit upon the head of Hyacinthus, and
killed him. Apollo out of the blood produced a
flower, which he called by the same name.

Apollo was the inventor and god of all the fine arts, of
medicine, music, poetry, and eloquence He received
from Jupiter the power of knowing futurity, and his
oracles were in repute through all the world his answers
were numerous, and he assumed various shapes to gratify
his passion

Zephyrus (the west wind) was said to produce flowers
and fruits by the sweetness of his breath. He had a
temple at Athens

EPITHALAMIUM.

—

" The Gnydian power."

Gnidus, (more properly Cnidus,) a city in Asia
Minor, where Venus was worshipped as the chief
deity.

" God of the fatal bow."

Cupid, the god of love, and Love itself, is
represented naked and winged, with a veil over
his eyes, and carrying a quiver upon his shoulders.
He holds a torch in one hand, and a bow with
darts in the other, wherewith he wounds the
hearts of lovers. He was worshipped with the
same solemnity as his mother, Venus.

" Nor Hymen, thou."

Among the Greeks, Hymen was the god of
marriage and of nuptial solemnities, at which he
was always supposed to attend. He was the son
of Apollo, and one of the Muses; hence the
allusion in the text to the place of his birth,
(Helicon)

" Upon the brow of tuneful mountain born."

Pancharis;

OR, THE

KISSES OF BONNEFONS.

PANCHARIS;

OR, THE

KISSES OF BONNEFONS.

—

KISS I.

NYMPH, all other nymphs excelling,
 On whose lips, so rosy bright,
All my hopes of bliss are dwelling,
 Source of every fond delight.

Gentle nymph, on whom is lavish'd
 Ev'ry sweet, enchanting grace,
Charms from other beauties ravish'd
 To adorn thy lovely face.

While my heart, with passion glowing,
 Calls thee loveliest, dearest, best,
Wilt thou, the soft kiss bestowing,
 Sooth its pains, and give it rest?

No, ah no! withhold the blessing,
  Keep the dang'rous boon away,
Lest its thrilling touch increasing
  Bid the flame more fiercely prey!

But thy lips to mine applying
  Gently steal my breath away,
Till with rapture fainting, dying,
  Ev'ry pulse forgets to play.

No, ah no! ev'n that were danger,
  And my soul might wing her flight,
And be, dearest girl, a ranger
  In those realms of endless night,

Where, condemn'd to gloom, and sadness,
  Plaintive spirits ever stray;
Where love ne'er cheers, nor mirth, nor gladness
  E'er beguile the ling'ring day.

Yet come! to mine thy lips applying
  Steal me from myself away,
Till with rapture fainting, dying,
  My soul, loos'd from these bonds of clay,

Hovers where in dark meanders
  Styx rolls on his lurid tide;
Where the soft Catullus wanders
  With Tibullus by his side.

I too in turn my lips applying
   Will gently steal thy honied breath,
Till thy soul, enraptur'd flying,
   Hastens to the realms beneath:

And in those bright regions hovers,
   Where so sweetly, side by side,
Undivided from their lovers,
   Nemesis, and Lesbia glide.

For within that realm of spirits
   Tend'rest joys await the bless'd;
Each his former love inherits—
   Still possessing still possess'd.

There, my lovely girl, I'll meet thee,
   Pale, and trembling on that coast,
And with rapt'rous kisses greet thee,
   Till, in silent wonder lost—

E'en those bards, whose gentle measures
   Told of bliss, and taught the way
Who o'er love's delightful treasures
   Held the undisputed sway—

All, with one accord, shall hail us
   Welcome to the blisful grove,
And confess that none excel us
   In the tender arts of love.

KISS II.

TO A NEEDLE THAT PRICKED HIS MISTRESS'S FINGER.

Ah! cruel instrument, declare
   What could thus induce thy spite
To wound the fingers of the fair,
   So soft, so delicate, and white?
What crime was theirs that they should bleed,
And thou commit the ruthless deed?

Inflict not thus the wanton smart
   On them as innocent as fair!
Go rather, and assail her heart,
   And deeply sate thy vengeance there—
That cruel heart that will not feel,
Senseless as adamant or steel.

For taught by thee the sense of pain
   She may relent, though cruel long:
No! 'tis not thine, and I in vain
   Exalt thy feeble powers in song:
How can thy fragile point assail
Where love's bright shafts could ne'er prevail?

KISS III.

TO HIS MISTRESS'S LAP-DOG.

Bless'd is thy lot, supremely bless'd,
  Who sees must envy thee;
Thus by that gentle hand caress'd,
And found on the rosy breast
  Of that fair queen of chastity.

Diverted by thy artless play,
  Companion of her home,
With thee she sports the live-long day,
And makes thee partner of her way
  When fancy leads her steps to roam.

Her daily meal she bids thee share,
  And, with unfeign'd delight,
Selecting, with attentive care,
The choicest morsels for thy fare,
  Provokes thy little appetite:

Then, when the sweet repast is o'er,
  Strives with new joys to bless:

Takes to her fragrant breast once more,
And kisses sweet, a balmy store,
  Her lips more prodigally press,

Than he, of such delights the sire,
  From Lesbia crav'd of old;
Catullus, whose sweet sounding lyre
Breath'd the soft notes of fond desire,
  And all love's tender raptures told.

Bless'd is thy lot, supremely bless'd
  With all love's sweetest store!
And is there whose insatiate breast,
With soft delights like thee possess'd,
  Would madly wish, and sigh for more?

And yet there is, by thee enjoy'd,
  E'en gods would give, to share,
The spangl'd heaven in which they pride,
Like thee to slumber by her side
  All the night long, and wanton there.

Sweet fav'rite, while 'tis thine to share
  What all with envy see:
For this her kindness, this her care,
Let gratitude reward the fair
  With pleasing, fond fidelity.

KISS IV.

UNHALLOW'D was the ruthless deed
'That made that rosy bosom bleed,
  Thou fell, remorseless thing!
For there has Venus made abode,
And there the little wanton god
  Waves blithe his golden wing.

Thou hast provok'd, in evil hour,
The wrath of each celestial pow'r
  On thy unholy head;
Graces, and Loves will all combine,
Insulted by this deed of thine,
  And signal vengeance shed.

But, oh! frown not on me, sweet fair,
For by those charming eyes I swear—
  Eyes that I value more
'Than the dear light that visits mine,
And by Cythera's holy shrine,
  And Love's almighty pow'r—

My heart partook not of the deed
'That made thy gentle bosom bleed;

Ah! no, I only sought
To snatch one dear delicious kiss,
But warm, and eager of the bliss,
　My mouth the mischief wrought.

Yet I'll confess the crime my own,
And let my penitence atone
　For the unhallow'd deed;
And, without murmur, to the weight
Of punishment, however great,
　Bow down my guilty head.

Yet, oh! frown not on me, sweet maid,
'Twas thy own loveliness betray'd,
　The fault was all thy own;
Hadst thou not been so passing fair,
Nor such temptations lur'd me ther.,
　The deed had ne'er been done.

KISS V.

TO HIS SOUL.

WHY thus fly to thy undoing
　Flutt'ring to the cruel fair?
There thou'lt meet with certain ruin
　Chains, and bondage wait thee there

In the lab'rinths of thy ringlets
  Love has wove a subtle chain,
Once entangled by thy winglets,
  None can set thee loose again:

Fruitless would be each endeavour,
  Vain will all thy struggles be ;
Thou must perish there, for never
  More canst thou return to me.

Yet I feel those eyes, that glancing
  From those lids so brightly play,
Like bewitching spells entrancing,
  Lure thee, foolish thing, away

From my heart I feel thee flying
  To that lip, and bosom fair ;
There in bliss thou wouldst be lying,
  But of those bright locks beware!

Treach'rous are those silken ringlets,
  There destruction waits for thee ;
And, entangled by thy winglets,
  Thou canst ne'er return to me.

KISS VI.

And woul'dst thou have me hide the smart
  That thrills in ev'ry aching vein,
And, with dissimulative art
  Conceal from all my inward pain?

Thou know'st not what the task would be
  Did fires like these within thee prey;
No, not all thy philosophy
  Could charm the urchin Love away.

Can I then gaze upon the light
  Of eyes that flash incessant fire,
And on those breasts so snowy white,
  Nor feel the pangs of fierce desire?

Can I behold each auburn tress
  That wantons round her lovely neck,
Lips that were surely made to bless,
  And th' rose that blooms on either cheek,

Nor deem e'en kingdoms cheaply lost
   For one short hour of rapt'rous bliss,
Give all that ever Ind' can boast
   To snatch one dear delicious kiss?

Perish the wretch that could behold
   Beauties like these with careless eye;
To all love's warmer raptures cold,
   Unheeded let him live, and die!

Why, let the mother, if she will,
   Watch careful of her daughter's fame,
And the dull husband, if he feel
   Suspicious of his wedded dame;

Though, whisper'd by the babbling crowd,
   My name be blaz'd through all the town,
Talk'd of in theatres aloud,
   Or e'en to gaping rustics known:

I care not for the mother's fear,
   Nor shun the jealous husband's eye;
Why, let them watch, and let them jeer,
   I joy in such publicity.

So liv'd our rugged sires of old,
   Ere Care receiv'd his cank'rous birth,
Those years were years of sterling gold,
   When good old Saturn rul'd the earth.

o

In all the glow of naked charms
  The fair one grac'd her lover's side,
Nor trembled then with fond alarms,
  For none was there who dared divide.

In converse sweet their days were pass'd,
  In gay delights and wanton wiles;
No clouds their heaven of love o'ercast,
  Nor fears disturb'd their rosy smiles.

Of dull decorum's rigid rules
  Let others boast, they're not for me;
I leave them to such whining fools:
  This—this is life from trammels free!

Why veil chaste Love in cold disguise,
  Such as he should not, cannot wear?
And why not let her incense rise
  At Venus' shrine, and worship there?

Is he who rules where planets shine,
  Are god themselves from failings free?
Lo! Phœbus and the god of wine,
  And the false Bull who cross'd the sea

Jove's tricks are known when he conceal'd
  His godhead in a swan's disguise;
And Hercules was forc'd to wield
  His distaff at a woman's voice.

Come then, we'll revel blithe and free.
　　Like gods, while glowing youth inspires;
If they could sin, then why should we
　　Blush to obey Love's tender fires?

KISS VII.

LET me kiss those soft lids, my dear joy,
　　Where those glances bewitchingly play;
Let me kiss those bright tresses that vie
　　With the god who illumines the day!

Ah! wouldst thou, ungrateful, deny
　　To thy poet so slight a request?
No, no, I can read in thine eye
　　The denial was only in jest.

Thou wouldst be but provokingly coy,
　　And seem to deny it to me;
With refusal enhance the sweet joy,
　　And tempt me to snatch it from thee.

6 2

Then thus in my arms will I fold thee,
  Thus circle that white neck of thine;
Thus—thus to my bosom I'll hold thee—
  And thus press those moist lips to mine.

Thou mayst pout, and look gloomy. and threat me
  And struggle to guard the dear bliss;
With scratches, and pinches beset me,
  While I snatch away kiss after kiss.

I'll fear not the threats thou mayst make,
  And laugh at each fruitless endeavour;
In my arms the more firmly I'll take,
  And kiss thee still closer than ever.

Oh! dearer to me are the joys
  That spring from sweet struggles like these,
For we deem it no longer a prize
  If we can enjoy when we please.

Then, oh! wouldst thou heighten the bliss,
  Thus ever, my Pancharis, fly me;
Thus, thus let me snatch the sweet kiss,
  Thus ever resist, and deny me.

KISS VIII.

Thou art sweet, yet with bitter alloy
  That sweetness is mingled in thee,
And thou art an object of joy
  As well as disquiet to me.

To me thou art like the fair star
  That beams when Aurora is nigh,
But changes its name, when night's car
  Is gloomy roll'd up on high.

Thou art light as when morn beams above,
  Yet dark as when the twilight's pass'd;
And now thou . . . . haven . . . thee,
  Now the . . . . on which I am cast.

Now like hope thy . . . . . can cheer,
  Now bid care and sorrow . . . :
To me thou'rt . . . . ,
  And yet I can hate . . . .

Thy faults and thy virtues to tell,
  The Muse might for e'er be inventing,
Few words would describe thee as well,
  So lovely, and yet so tormenting.

KISS IX.

Give me, sweet life, the kiss that's rife
  With honied moisture sweet,
That will assuage the fires that rage
  With such consuming heat;

And with the dew that doth imbue
  Thy lips so ruby bright,
Bid them allay the flames that play
  Within me day and night.

Ah! no, forbear, my gentle fair,
  I know not what I sue;
Oh! keep away from me, I pray,
  Those lips that would undo,

And fan the fire of fierce desire,
  Till, glowing in my heart,
O'er all my soul the torrents roll,
  Consuming ev'ry part.

Why snatch from me so hastily
  The lip that presses mine?
Oh! come, and pour the burning shower
  Of kisses all from thine.

Let me expire by their sweet fire,
   Till, from each burning kiss,
Like him I rise, who to the skies
   From Œta soar'd to bliss.

———

KISS X.

How can two such extremes consent,
   Dear maid, in thee ;
That when such sweetness all is thine,
   Sweeter than sweet can be,
Thy lips such bitterness impart,
And from thine eyes envenom'd arrows dart ?

But when thou art so bitter all,
   To such degree
That all the bitterness of gall
   Cannot be equal thee ;
Why are thy kisses then so sweet,
And with ambrosial dews thy lips replete?

Why do the glances of thine eyes
   No longer sting,
But with each shaft that from them flies
   Such gentle pleasures bring ?

Is't in thy lips, I pr'ythee, tell,
Or in thy glances that such virtues dwell:

That thus at times my soul they bless
    With bitter joy,
And now with honied bitterness
    Oppress me and destroy!
Oh! bitterness too cloying sweet;
Oh! sweet with too much bitterness replete?

———

KISS XI.

Ah! wherefore is thy lot so bless'd,
    Sweet, pretty blossom,
Thus in the inmost folds to rest
    Of that dear, lovely bosom?
Oh! were it mine like thee to share
The rosy heaven that beams so brightly there

Thrice happy flow'ret! not like thee
    Tranquil I'd lie,
But wand'ring unconstrain'd, and free,
    To all her beauties fly;
And burning kisses o'er and o'er,
On her fair neck and tender bosom pour.

Now I'd intently gaze where rise
    Those hills of snow,
Examining with curious eyes
    The fairest of the two;
And then, by turns, from that to this,
My playful lips should rove, and print the kiss:

Then hide me in the rosy vale
    That lies between,
And 'twixt them softly gliding steal
    Where beauties blush unseen;
There ev'ry secret charm I'd spy,
And none should 'scape love's penetrating eye.

But, ah! sweet blossom, not for me
    Are those dear joys,
And what, unask'd, she gives to thee,
    To me she e'er denies:
Not e'en my lips may come
To lightly touch, or hands to wander there.

While thou, unconscious of the blessing,
    Liest there unmov'd,
On her dear breast those joys possessing
    That only thou hast prov'd;
'Tis mine at distance to admire,
And sigh, and look, and kindle with desire.

KISS XII.

Go thou, my heart, but swiftly go,
   And tell the cruel fair what fires
With scorching heat consume thee now,
   What num'rous griefs, what fond desires
Tell her my tears, with ceaseless flow,
   Bedew my cheeks, and swollen eyes,
And life itself becomes a woe,
   Nor finds relief in fruitless sighs.

Yet 'midst those daily tears that steep
   My pallid cheeks, those fires that glow
With ceaseless rage, and bid me weep
   In wan despair o'er all my woe;
Bid her the kind assurance give
   She'll yet bestow a thought on me,
And hope again will bid me live,
   And peace return, and dwell with thee.

KISS XIII.

As when some comet blazes in the skies
The gather'd people view with wond'ring eyes;

Trembling, they deem their race already run,
And all the horrors of the war begun;
Surprise and terror seize on ev'ry mind,
And all foredoom the ruin of their kind:
So when the maid, in dazzling beauty bright,
As fair, as lovely as yon orb of light,
Bursts forth to view, all silently they gaze,
In admiration lost, and mute amaze:
Trembling they see, and fear that mischief lies
In the bright glances of her beaming eyes:
In ev'ry bosom throb these soft alarms;
And now they dread, and now admire her charms
And, while their fear increases as they view,
Tremble to think what ruin may ensue.

KISS XIV.

Away! for no longer I prize thee,
  Thy love and thy beauty I spurn,
To the girl who so proudly denies me
  I too can be proud in my turn.

Thou hast taught me to know that 'tis folly
  To hope any more from thy pride,
Now I'll laugh, and turn from thee as coolly
  As thou when my suit was denied.

Away! for no longer the muses
    Shall pour their soft notes to thy praise:
No, no, for the girl who abuses
    Shall ne'er win a name by my lays.

Go, herd with thy favourite throng,
    A vulgar and ignorant crew ;
I should blush was thy name in my song,
    So, false one, I bid thee adieu!

Thou dost proudly reject, and despise me,
    But yet there is one who will prove
There still beats a heart that can prize me,
    A heart that can cherish and love.

She is lovely, and fair as the blossom
    That smiles when the summer is near;
Turilla will take to her bosom,
    And be, what thou was not, sincere.

To her, while my soft notes I'm thrilling,
    And with pleasure she lists to the strain,
Thou wilt grieve that thy place she is filling,
    And sigh to possess me again.

KISS XV.

PROPITIOUS chance, my friend, betray'd
Where, like a Naiad sporting in the wave,
  My love, beneath the leafy shade
To the cool, sparkling stream her beauties gave;

Unconscious of my gaze she stood,
While all her naked limbs of glowing white
  So sweetly through the lucid flood,
With soft'ned graces, struggle I into sight:

That beauteous neck was all confess'd,
Fair as pale winter's garb of fleecy snows;
  And wildly the alternate breast
Before my view in ripe luxuriance rose;

Firm as two little globes they seem'd
From Parian marble shap'd by skilful hands;
  Or like the ruby's light they gleam'd,
When fixed in gold the glitt'ring jewel stands:

Not milky streams so purely white,
Nor the first snows that wint'ry tempests bring;
  And sweetly tip'd with rosy light
Like strawb'rries blushing through their leaves in
    spring.

By turns the varying colours spread,
Mingling the lily with the blushing rose;
  Or like the hues of that bright red
Which Tyrian purple o'er fair ivory throws.

  Reflected by the lucid waves
Her glowing beauties beam'd with mellower light·
  So seems, when in the virgin stream she laves
Her virgin form, the goddess of the night.

  More had I seen, but the rude breeze
Shook the dark foliage with its passing breath,
  And startled by the rustling trees,
Deep blushing at herself, she plung'd beneath.

KISS XVI.

An! wherefore fly sweet nymph, why breathless
    run
To shades and thickets, and my converse shun?
Oh! seek not shelter there. so me clown may meet,
And thy soft form with ruthless freedom treat;
Clasp thy fair neck, or kiss thy blushing cheek,
And e'en thy fiercest struggles prove too weak.

Thy truth I fear not. no 'tis love misgives—
Love in a true breast seldom ever lives;
Health, youth, and vigour in these limbs combine,
Glow in each pulse, and in my features shine;
Why then suspect that thou couldst yield those
    charms
To some mean rustic's rude, ungentle arms,
Or to some dotard's, in whose pulses flow
Life's freezing currents languishing, and slow.
Ah' no, though not to please thee be my fate,
And though thou shunn'st, I feel thou dost not
    hate.
Beware, ye clowns, nor touch the maid I love,
Far, far, from her attacks I both remove;
Touch not with sacrilegious hands the fair,
Mine, mine she is, unmanner'd clowns, forbear!

    But wherefore dost thou fly, why breathless
    run
To shades and thickets, and my converse shun?
Yet fly, thy footsteps, to affection true,
Thro' woods, thro' wilds, o'er deserts I'd pursue;
Swim the deep river, climb the steepest height,
Face ev'ry danger, and press to the fight;
Even though the North his utmost fury shed
In sleety show'rs on my uncover'd head;
Though the fierce Dog-star rage, or frost, and snow
Arrest the foaming torrents as they flow:

These aave no terrors in a lover's eyes,
They but increase, and bid his courage rise,
And with a willing heart he dares each enterprize.

Yes, I believe thou dost not, canst not hate,
And doubt yet fear, would learn yet dread my fate;
Hope still persuades that 'twill be mine no more
On night's dull ear my plaintive voice to pour;
Nor mourn in shades, and with my tale of love
Weary the babbling echoes of each grove;
No more pursue thy flight, with trembling feet,
Through winter's cold, and summer's scorching
      heat;
Nor keep my vigils when with silv'ry light
No friendly planet cheers the gloom of night.
Oh! be these past, the painful labour spare,
And cease thy cruel flight, divinely fair!
Scorn'd are my pray'rs, unheeded are my cries,
Oh! hapless fate, see still she flies, she flies
And shall thy tyranny be never past,
And these thy torments, Love, for ever last?

KISS XVII.

WHILE round thee my fond arms I twine,
And press my glowing lips to thine,

And eager of the bliss inhale
The balmy breath's nectareous gale;
Lost in the ecstasies of love,
I seem to soar in worlds above,
And seem, my fair one, seem to be
E'en happier than divinity.

But when, with tantalizing charms,
Thou break'st from these encircling arms,
Hurl'd from those fairy realms of bliss,
I'm plung'd to hell's profound abyss,
In horrors lost, and deeper woe
Than spirits in that world below.

———

KISS XVIII

SILLY thing, in search of bliss,
 Didst thou dare to touch her lip,
And in each nectarous kiss
 Balmy dews of nectar sip?

Tempt the sweet repast no more,
 For in ev'ry kiss's breath,
While thou sipp'st the honied store,
 Deadly poisons lurk beneath.

M

Though the liquid ardours flow
  Swiftly through each vital part,
Till in ev'ry pulse they glow,
  And consume thy aching heart;

Still, unmindful of the past,
  To her ruby lips thou fliest,
And there madly dar'st to taste
  Th' honied bliss by which thou diest.

In those lips of rosy hue
  Pain, and pleasure mingled lie;
Oh! how sweetly they undo,
  By how many arts destroy.

Fair destroyers of my peace,
  Why so many pangs impart?
Cease those fiery torments, cease,
  And no more distract my heart.

Give me sweets, but give them pure;
  When I seek the balmy kiss
Let me sip, but sip secure,
  Nor with tortures taint the bliss,

KISS XIX.

Oh! lovely are those locks that stray
  In ringlets o'er thy forehead fair,
And lovelier the bright eyes that play
  So wildly glancing here and there:

Oh! lovely are those breasts that vie
  With hers whom Cupid calls his mother,
And in their snow-white purity
  Seem to out-rival one another:

Sweet are those lips so ruby bright,
  Like twin rosebuds in vernal weather
When their young beauties burst in sight:
  Oh! thou art lovely altogether.

Would that those locks had lost their brightness,
  Those eyes the fires that in them play;
Those lips their hue, those breasts their whiteness
  And thou, O thou! been far away.

Not then my luckless glance had lighted,
  And gaz'd upon the beauteous whole;
Not then my peace had thus been blighted,
  Nor blank despair have seiz'd my soul.

H 2

KISS XX.

Ye pearly tears, whose falling showers
　Deck her fair cheeks with many a gem,
Like dew-drops on the queen of flowers
　Ere the sun's light hath scatter'd them;

Why 'neath your sparkling drops conceal
　Fires that with sudden flashes play,
And, as with silent course they steal,
　Mischief to every heart convey?

No, no, the silv'ry streams that flow,
　And glitter on thy cheeks, my fair,
Cannot be tears, but fires that glow,
　And dart their flashes ev'ry where.

Deep, deep, in ev'ry vital part
　By me their thrilling force is felt;
Swiftly through ev'ry pulse they dart,
　And my poor heart consume and melt.

What have not lovers now to fear,
　If elements with thee conspire;
If flames commingle in a tear,
　And fire be water, water fire.

KISS XXI.

Au! whither have ye led,
  Ye faithless messengers of love,
And ere I could suspect betray'd?
  Ye wantons, what could move
You thus to fix my aching sight
  On charms that beam'd so bright,
That dazzled with excess of light
  In giddy trance my senses fled away?
  Ye too, as treacherous as they,
My feet, why did ye bear my weight
  Where dwells the unrelenting fair,
To sue in vain before her gate,
  And overcome with sorrow perish there?
  My wanton hands, why did ye dare
To press those little hills of snow?
    Instant through ev'ry vein
    The subtle poison ran,
In ev'ry pulse I feel it throb, and glow;
And deeply lodg'd within my heart,
'T will burn for ever there, and mock the aid of art.

  On you will I avenge the wrong.
  And curb your wantonness!

My feet, no longer shall ye rove,
For many a chain secure, and strong
  That restless spirit shall repress,
And keep ye from the fair's abode.
You too with manacles I'll load,
My wanton hands, and ye shall prove
  The utmost my revenge can do;
    For e'er debarr'd access,
    Ye never more shall press
With wanton touch the charms that led you there.
  But, oh! my faithless eyes, for you
Vengeance more deep will I prepare;
A gloomy covering shall confine
    And veil ye from the light;
    Thus plung'd in endless night,
Ye never more shall fix my aching sight
On beauties that so dangerously shine.

KISS XXII.

CEASE, tormentor, cease to grieve me;
  Tyrant, wilt thou ne'er give o'er,
Never from these fires relieve me?
  Sighs but bid them rage the more—

Fan the flame, increase the anguish,
  Till in ev'ry pulse they glow :
With their force, I faint, I languish,
  Cease, nor more torment me so !

Flow, my tears, nor cease your flowing
  Till you've set my heart at rest ;
And to one vast torrent growing
  Quench at once the raging pest !
Vainly is my soul imploring
  Aid ye can no more supply ;
For those fires, for e'er devouring,
  Every source, alas ! is dry.

KISS XXIII.

Where the wild woods were waving green
  My steps by chance were straying,
While the deceitful maid, unseen,
  Many a snare was laying ;
As thoughtless by I rov'd along
  She caught my heart so clever ;
Vainly I strove, her nets were strong,
  'Twas caught, alas ! for ever.

Ah me! I cried, ungrateful fair,
    Why cruelly deceive me ;
And with such treacherous arts ensnare,
    And of my heart bereave me?
I sigh not that 'tis now with thee,
    It is not that, believe me ;
But thou hast stol'n the heart from me
    Which I had meant to give thee.

— — — —

KISS XXIV.

'Twas noon, and to my fair's abode
    My pensive way I took,
When sudden from a lurid cloud
    The fearful tempest broke ;
The thunders roll'd, the lightning play'd,
    When, with disorder'd charms,
And all a woman's fears, the maid
    Sought shelter in my arms.

Save me! oh, save! she wildly cried,
    And threw her on my breast ;
While all a lover's arts I tried,
    And to my bosom press'd.

Dear, little trembler, wherefore fly
   For safety to my arms ;
And while the tempest rolls on high
   Thus shake with vain alarms?

Why wouldst thou have me shield thee here,
   On this fond bosom laid,
When I alone have cause of fear,
   And most require thine aid?
More dang'rous are those beaming eyes,
   There fiercer lightnings play,
And the rude storm that rends the skies
   Less to be fear'd than they.

KISS XXV.

DIFF'RING flowers in the wreath I send,
      Dear maid, unite ;
Their hues two blooming roses blend,
      The scarlet, and the white :
In the one thine eyes may trace
The pallid emblem of my love-sick face ;
   Th' other's fiery tints portray
The heart that cruel love has made his prey.

KISS XXVI.

Oh! those eyes are bewitchingly bright,
   They glance but too surely to kill;
And yet for a while would I borrow their light,
   And brandish their fires at my will.

Would you ask why such weapons I sue,
   With mischief so heavily fraught;
These fires would I lance, my dear charmer, at you,
   And show you the ills they have wrought.

KISS XXVII.

ON A PICTURE OF HIS MISTRESS.

Bless'd was the limner's hands that bade
   Those features on thy surface shine,
And with advent'rous skill portray'd
    That form, and made thee what thou art,
     divine:
  And heav'n-born was the art that made thee bear
Those eyes, and that fair face that have no equals
   here.

What though the Coan artist drew,
  And Venus gave to mortal eye,
A thousand such as thee in view,
  And thy bright tints with his may safely vie:
Immodest beauties from his pencil shine,
But thou art chasteness all, and purer charms are
    thine.

What though the huge Colossus rears
  Above fair Rhodes his towering height,
And on his giant forehead bears
  The image of yon glorious orb of light;
A thousand suns in thee as brightly gleam,
Those eyes are suns to me, and shed as bright a
    beam.

KISS XXVIII.

Think not those glancing orbs of light,
That look so fair and beam so bright
    Are only eyes:
Ah! no, the god of rage's fiercest gleam
Is centred in their ev'ry beam,
And thence, on fatal mischief bent,
Full many a fiery shaft is sent,
    And he that meets them dies.

KISS XXIX.

I WOULD not have the girl I love
   In sparkling gems array'd;
I would not have her proudly move
   In silks or stiff brocade:

No diamonds should adorn her head,
   Or glitter round her neck;
Nor vile cosmetics idly spread
   Their poison o'er her cheek.

The modest look, the artless air
   Best heighten ev'ry grace;
And the pure blush that mantles there
   Sheds lustre o'er her face:

The gairish gem, the stiffen'd dress
   But spoil the easy mien,
And art, while it makes each beauty less,
   Hides graces better seen.

KISS XXX.

Oh! love is a treacherous boy,
  See, see, how the truant deceives me,
That she lov'd me she swore by on high,
  And now for another she leaves me.

How false, and how faithless is woman,
  From fancy to fancy still ranging ;
Her heart can be constant to no man,
  But day after day will be changing.

For did she not vow, o'er and o'er,
  That mine she would be, and for ever
Oh! did she not swear by each power,
  That death, only death, should dissever ?

'Tis not for the vows she had plighted,
  Now shamelessly broken, I sigh ;
That I leave to the gods she has slighted,
  And they may avenge it on high.

But thus to forsake him whose pride
  Thou wast, on thy beauty who doted;
Leave him for a soldier's mean bride,
  And fly from a heart so devoted—

The heart that was worth thy caressing,
  Whose pleasure was but to obey;
And that heart thou mightst still be possessing,
  Still proud to acknowledge thy sway.

He may love, but he will not, believe me,
  Thus glory in wearing thy chain;
Yet this bosom, though thou couldst deceive me
  And scorn me, will love thee again.

Yes, yes, even now 'twill adore thee,
  And swear to obey thee once more;
Do thou but consent to restore me
  The heart that thou gav'st me before.

If thou canst not restore it again,
  And thy cruelty will not be mov'd,
Smile on me, and spare me the pain
  To think that I cannot be lov'd.

KISS XXXI.

TO HIS POEMS.

THEN go, since ye avail me nough·
  And have betray'd a lover;
Burn for the mischief ye have wrought,
  For now ye cannot move her.
What would it boot, though fame proming,
  And after ages read it,
If still unsoften'd by his song
  Is she for whom he made it?
Go burn, for ye have wrong'd my truth,
  And prov'd my own undoing;
Go, perish, like my hopes of youth,
  In yonder fiery ruin.

And yet ye were the tender gage
  Of love when first beginning;
And shall I, in my senseless rage,
  Condemn, without repining,
The verse that tells how pure the flame
  That in my heart was lighted,
And still retains her dear lov'd name
  To whom those vows were plighted?

No, no, though ye've undone my youth,
　And all my hopes have perish'd,
Ye were the pledges once of truth,
　Live on, and still be cherish'd.

———

KISS XXXII.

THOUGH the sky be o'ercast,
　And the rain fall fast,
It will not incessantly pour;
　Though the wild winds rave
　O'er the dark-blue wave,
It's face will be smooth when the tempest is o'er

　But the show'rs that rise
　In these tear-swoln eyes
Keep flowing, and never will cease;
　And still o'er my soul
　Care's billows will roll,
And pity's soft calm never hush them to peace.

　Though the wide vault of heaven,
　By thunders be riven,

Each bolt to the earth will not dart;
    But more dang'rous ti an they
    Are the bright eyes that play,
And incessantly pierce with their flashes my heart.

    From his feast of gore
    The vulture gives o'er,
To the Titan's keen pangs giving rest;
    But by night and by day,
    Love ne'er quits his prey,
And still darts his torturing fangs through my
       breast.

    E'en the punishing wheel
    Of Ixion stands still,
And Sisyphus rests from his stone;
    But from cares that molest
    This heart knows no rest,
They still will perplex it, and never have done.

    Oh! sad was the light
    Of the star that night,
That beam'd at the hour of my birth;
    And the heav'ns look'd down
    With their darkest frown,
Nor smil'd on the day that produc'd me on earth.

KISS XXXIII.

I MOURN not that the soft melodious tone
   Of thy sweet voice hath, like enchantment, reft
   My ev'ry sense, or that my soul has left
This feeble clay untenanted, and flown
To join in pleasing dalliance with thine own,
   Lur'd from me by thy moist lips when I quaff'd
   Of dewy kisses the ambrosial draught.
Nor that my foolish heart from me hath gone
To dwell with thee: ah! no, I only sigh
   To think that when, with fast receding breath
In the delirious trance of ecstasy,
   My spirit hovers on the brink of death,
'Twill not at that dear moment wholly fly,
And let me in thy fond embraces sweetly die.

———

KISS XXXIV.

FAIREST of blossoms, on whose lips the rose
   Hath left its sweetness, from the wanton
      wreaths
Of whose bright ringlets, and whose bosom flowy
   Fragrance like that the vernal violet breathes,

Or the od'rous shrubs of Araby exhale,
Flinging their spicy sweets on ev'ry passing gale:

Come, breathe them from thy lips, and gently
    press
    On mine the honied dews of many a kiss,
Rapt'rous, and warm with love, and numberless;
    Like young doves be our interchange of bliss,
And not like her, the Roman maid of old,
Who counted the sweet store—Oh! be not thou
    so cold.

Come, dearest, with thy smiling lips apart
    Pouring a show'r of kisses sweet, then
Them closer still, and from thy inmost heart
    Breathe forth thy soul, and let it mix with
    mine:
But mingle so that never art shall sever.
And like our endless love be thus conjoin'd for
    ever.

KISS XXXV.

Then hear me, goddess, thou whose care benign
    Guards watchful o'er the lover's destiny,
    If, when again in am'rous ecstasy

On her fair bosom breathless I recline,
Life should forsake this feeble frame of mine,
   And my frail spirit bursts her bonds of clay;
   For such may yet arrive, when slow decay
Hath weaken'd every barrier; be it thine,
Sweet pow'r, to guide the disembodied sprite
   To thy fair mansions, where for ever reign,
In sunny regions of celestial light,
   Laughter and mirth, and joy unmix'd with pain
There, in the green recesses of the bless'd,
Lull'd in Elysian raptures let me rest.

PERVIGILIUM VENERIS.

ALL hail! thou dear delicious night,
   Ye silent hours of darkness, hail!
Not day so welcome to my sight
As the soft shadows of your dusky veil:

For, borne upon your raven wing,
   Love, and love's dear delights ye bring,
     Replete with tender joy:

And when your friendly shades are near
The girl, reliev'd of half her fear,
  Grows less severe, and coy.

    Now thou art mine,
    And I am thine,
  Now, now, sweet maid, I hold thee;
Now my fond arms around thee twine,
  And to my bosom fold thee.

Now to thee the joyous rite,
  Laughter-loving queen, we'll pay,
And with raptures sweet requite
The teasing cares of many a dull delay.

  Why a prey to torments leave me,
  Sweet seducer, why deceive me?
  While in blushes o'er thy cheeks
  Love so eloquently speaks;
  Reflected by thy sparkling eyes
  While my am'rous wishes rise;
  Why not let me fondly twine
  Round that lovely neck of thine,
  And mouth to mouth, and lip to lip
  Soul-entrancing kisses sip?
Still, to thy virgin fears a prey,
  Thou wouldst fly my circling arms,
And turn thy blushing cheeks away,
While sweet confusion heightens all thy charms.

By those piercing orbs of light,
By those lips so ruby bright:
By thy cheeks, and by the hair
That wantons o'er thy forehead fair;
By those little breasts of snow
 Where such sweet temptations dwell,
And like two gems that brightly glow,
 In all their ripe luxuriance swell—
Oh! spare, and leave me not a prey
  To the fierce fire
  Of wild desire:
Soon will my spirit wing her way
 Unequal to the strife,
Unless thy balmy breath allay,
 And call me back to life.
Aid me, thou rosy queen of joy,
And thou, O love's delicious boy,
For raging now with fierce control
The fiery torments madden all my souL

Thus, with fast-receding breath,
And gasping on the brink of death,
In the wild accents of despair
With many a sigh I pour'd my pray'r.
To pity mov'd, at length the maid
 Forgot her tender fears;
Her cheeks the rosy blush o'erspread,
 And smiling through her tears,

Thine will I be, she sweetly cried,
And threw her on my breast,
And her moist lips to mine appli d,
And dewy kisses press'd;
Thine will I be, she cried, and bol'er grown,
Sought my fond arms, and press'd me in her own.

A golden bed
Beneath us spread,
There clasp'd in many a fold,
While bashfully she struggled yet,
My arms the blushing wanton hold.
And lips by lips so sweetly met,
I revel in the balmy bliss
Of many a dear delicious kiss:
Now with her limbs my limbs entwine,
My mouth to her's now fondly join;
Then in search of sweets I rove
To those dear retreats of love,
Where smiling Venus holds her court,
And little Loves around her sport;
Those ruby lips where roses bloom,
And violets scatter sweet perfume:
There, while entranc'd with rapt'rous joy
I snatch delicious kisses,
Young Love beholds with jealous eye,
And envies all my blisses:

While lips meet lips in melting twine,
Sweetly our mingling spirits join,
And lost in joyous dreams of ecstasy we lie.

Oh, happy bed! oh, happy night!
Ye silent witnesses of dear delight—
When in my fond encircling arms
To my warm breast I clasp'd her glowing
     charms,
And read within her melting eye
The future pledge of many a rapt'rous joy;
While lip met lip in am'rous play,
And sweetly struggling snatch'd the kiss
     away,
Till limb with limb entwin'd in pleasing trance
    we lay.

Avaunt! ye tenants of the sky,
In thrilling ecstasy I cry;
Not all your bright Olympian bowers,
   Not rich ambrosial dews,
   Nor nectar's sparkling juice,
Can yield such dear delights as ours!
And while such sweets to me are given,
Unenvied be your spangled heaven;
Let but these longing arms of mine
Around her beauteous neck entwine:

Oh! let me but securely sip
The honey of her ruby lip,
And gaze, with fond impassion'd eye,
Upon those tender breasts that vie
  With hers whom Cupid calls his mother,
And in their snow-white purity
  So sweetly rival one another :—
Then, down the rosy vale that lies between,
Steal on to beauties yet unseen,
Where, in silent ambush laid,
  Sly Cupid guards the secret treasure,
  And the rosy queen of pleasure
Revels in the pleasing shade.
Thus limb from limb so fondly twin'd,
We give to rapture all the mind,
And kisses told by thousands o'er
On each other's lips we pour;
And, like lulling turtle-doves,
Interchange our rapt'rous loves,
        'Till breathless quite
        With wild delight,
On her gently heaving breast,
In thrilling transports lost, I sink to balmy rest.

There, while in pleasing trance I lay,
And ev'ry pulse forgot to play—
Oh! sleep you so, she sweetly cried—
Oh! sleep you so, and by my side?

And now my hand she gently press'd,
Now lightly touch'd my panting breast;
And now with many a dewy kiss,
Recall'd my soul to life, and bliss.
I clasp'd her in my arms once more,
And kiss'd the wanton o'er and o'er;
From joy to joy we swiftly pas 'd
    Till fled the shades of night;
Morning surpris'd our joys at last,
    And pour'd the unwelcome light.

All hail! thou dear delicious night,
    Ye silent hours of darkness hail!
Ye harbingers of dear light,
Welcome, thrice welcome is your shadowy veil.

NOTES

KISSES OF BONNEFONS.

— —

KISS I.

"Where the soft Catullus wanders
With Tibullus by his side."

Catullus, a Roman poet, whose compositions, elegant and simple, are the offspring of a luxuriant imagination. Tibullus, also a Roman poet, composed elegant love-verses in praise of his mistresses. (See Neærea.)

"Nemesis and Lesbia glide."

The Greeks celebrated a festival called Nemesia, in memory of deceased persons, as the goddess Nemesis was supposed to defend the relics and the memory of the dead, from all insult. For an account of **Lesbia,** see Notes to "Kisses of Secundus."

KISS IV.

"Graces and Loves will all combine."

Aglaia, Thalia, and Euphrosyne, are the names of the Graces. They are generally represented with their hands joined together.

———

KISS VI.

" Good old Saturn rul'd the earth."

Saturn and Janus were the kings of Italy. Saturn's reign was so mild and popular, so beneficent and virtuous, that mankind have called it the golden age, to intimate the happiness and tranquillity which the earth then enjoyed.

"Jove's tricks are known when he conceal'd
    His godhead in a swan's disguise;
And Hercules was forc'd to wield
    His distaff at a woman's voice."

Jupiter (Jove) was king of heaven; but his peaceful reign was disturbed by the giants, who, however, with the assistance of Hercules, he totally vanquished. Jupiter assumed many shapes in order to gratify his passions. He introduced himself to Danae in a shower of gold; he corrupted Antiope in the form of a satyr; and Leda in the form of a swan, he became a bull to seduce Europa; and he enjoyed the company of Ægina in the form of a flame of fire. He was the father of the Graces, the Seasons, and the Muses.

Hercules was doomed by his father to be subservient to his mother, which natural right she cruelly exercised. She imposed upon him the most dangerous and uncommon enterprises, well known by the name of the twelve labours of Hercules. The fifty daughters of the king of Thespis became mothers by Hercules, during his stay of fifty days at Thespis, though some say it was all effected in one night.

KISS IX.

"From Œta soar'd to bliss."

Œta, a celebrated mountain between Thessaly and Macedonia, upon which Hercules burnt himself.

KISS XV.

" Where like a Naiad sporting in the wave."

Naiades, certain inferior deities who presided over rivers, springs, and fountains.

———

KISS XXVII.

"What though the Coan artist drew."

Apelles was the celebrated painter of Cos. He lived in the age of Alexander the Great, and was in great favour with him. He painted a naked Venus rising out of the sea. He also painted a picture of Alexander, which the king did not approve of; a horse, however, passing by neighed at the horse in the piece, when the painter observed, "One would imagine that the horse is a better judge of painting than your majesty."

" What though the huge Colossus rears."

Colossus, a celebrated brazen image at Rhodes; one of the seven wonders of the world. It was feet high, and every thing in equal proportion. Ships have passed full sail between its legs.

KISS XXXII.

" Of Ixion stands still
Aud Sisyphus rests from his stone."

Jupiter took Ixion up into heaven, where the latter would have ravished Juno; but Jupiter formed a cloud in her shape, on which Ixion begat the Centaurs: (half men and half horses.) Ixion, for boasting he had been with Juno, was cast down to hell, where he was tied to a wheel in perpetual motion.

Sisyphus was condemned in hell to roll to the top of a hill a large stone, which had no sooner reached the summit, than it fell back into the plain with impetuosity, and rendered his punishment eternal. Various causes have been assigned for this rigorous sentence; the more favoured opinion, however, is, that he received permission to revisit the earth to punish his wife for having buried his body, but that he violated his engagement, and therefore was doomed to endless labour

Kisses:

BY

VARIOUS AUTHORS.

KISSES:

BY

VARIOUS AUTHORS.

—

I.

CATULLUS.

As many stellar eyes of light
As through the silent waste of night,
Gazing upon this world of shade,
Witness some secret youth and maid,
Who, fair as thou and fond as I,
In stolen joys enamour'd lie!
So many kisses, ere I slumber,
Upon those dew-bright lips I'll number·
So many vermil, honied kisses,
Envy can never count our blisses.
No tongue shall tell the sum but mine
No lips shall fascinate but thine'

KISSES.

II.

LONGEPIERRE.

FLY, my belov'd, to yonder stream,
We'll plunge us from the noontide beam;
Then cull the rose's humid bud,
And dip it in our goblet's flood.
Our age of bliss, my nymph, shall fly,
As sweet, though passing as that sigh,
Which seems to whisper o'er your lip,
"Come, while you may, of rapture sip!"
For age will steal the rosy form,
And chill the pulse which trembles warm;
And death—alas! that hearts, which thrill
Like yours and mine, should e'er be still.

———

III.

T. MOORE.

TAKE back the sigh, thy lips of art
    In passion's moment breath'd to me
Yet, no—it must not, will not part,
'Tis now the life-breath of my heart,
    And has become too pure for thee.

Take back the kiss, that faithless sigh
  With all the warmth of truth imprest;
Yet, no—the fatal kiss may lie,
Upon thy lip its sweets would die,
  Or bloom to make a rival blest.

Take back the vows that, night and day,
  My heart receiv'd, I thought, from thine;
Yet, no—allow them still to stay,
They might some other heart betray,
  As sweetly as they've ruin'd mine.

IV.

[From the German.]

The kiss that you press'd on my lip
  Has but kindl'd more fiercely the fire
And e'en gods 'midst their raptures would weep
  Did they burn as I do with desire;

For scarce had my soul felt the bliss
  When you left me to mourn that 't was given
Is this to impart the sweet kiss,
  The nectar they boast of in heaven?

No, no; ah! believe me, 't is merely
　　To sharpen the stings of desire,
And make me but feel more severely
　　The tortures by which I expire.

So feels, when thirst parches his lip,
　　The traveller to whom rustics tell
Of the cool sparkling stream he may sip,
　　Yet refuse him access to the well.

———

V.

MENAGE.

As dancing o'er the enamell'd plain,
The flow'ret of the virgin train,
My soul's Corinna lightly play'd,
Young Cupid saw the graceful maid;
He saw, and in a moment flew,
And round her neck his arms he threw;
And said, with smiles of infant joy,
"Oh! kiss me, mother, kiss thy boy!"
Unconscious of a mother's name,
The modest virgin blush'd with shame
And angry Cupid, scarce believing
That vision could be so deceiving,

Thus to mistake his Cyprian dame.
The little infant blush'd with shame.
"Be not asham'd, my boy," I cried,
For I was ling'ring by his side:
"Corinna and thy lovely mother,
Believe me, are so like each other,
That clearest eyes are oft betray'd,
And take thy Venus for the maid."

———

VI.

T. MOORE.

BEHOLD, my love, the curious gem
  Within this simple ring of gold;
'T is hallow'd by the touch of them
  Who liv'd in classic hours of old.

Some fair Athenian girl, perhaps,
  Upon her hand this gem display'd,
Nor thought that time's eternal lapse
  Should see it grace a lovelier maid.

Look, darling, what a sweet design,
  The more we gaze, it charms the more:
Come,—closer bring that cheek to mine,
  And trace with me its beauties o'er.

Thou seest it is a simple youth
     By some enamour'd nymph embrac'd
Look, Nea, love, and say in sooth
     Is not her hand most dearly plac'd?

Upon his curled head behind
     It seems in careless play to lie,
Yet presses gently, half inclin'd
     To bring his lip of nectar nigh.

Oh! happy maid, too happy boy;
     The one so fond and faintly loth,
The other yielding slow to joy—
     Oh! rare indeed, but blissful both.

Imagine, love, that I am he,
     And just as warm as he is chilling;
Imagine, too, that thou art she,
     But quite as cold, as she is willing:

So may we try the graceful way
     In which their gentle arms are twin'd,
And thus, like her, my hand I lay
     Upon thy wreathed hair behind:

And thus I feel thee breathing sweet,
     As slow to mine thy head I move;
And thus our lips together meet,
     And—thus I kiss thee—oh, my love'

VII.

SAPPHO.

Hither, Venus' queen of kisses,
This shall be the night of blisses;
This the night, to friendship dear,
Thou shalt be our Hebe here.
Fill the golden brimmer high,
Let it sparkle like thine eye;
Bid the rosy current gush,
Let it mantle like thy blush.
Venus! hast thou e'er above
Seen a feast so rich in love?
Not a soul that is not mine!
Not a soul that is not thine!

———

VIII.

MOSCHUS.

On him, who the haunts of my Cupid can show,
A kiss of the tenderest stamp I'll bestow;
But he, who can bring me the wanderer here,
Shall have something more rapt'rous, something
    more dear.

IX.

[From the French.]

WHILE you incline that neck of snow
To ev'ry kiss my lips bestow,
And in those passion-beaming eyes
Such inexpressive meaning lies.
Enraptur'd by the kindling glance
My soul dissolves in am'rous trance,
And on your gently heaving breast
Exanimate I sink to rest.

But when our lips, in wanton play,
So sweetly kiss for kiss repay,
And from that humid panting lip
Such sweet, such balmy dews I sip,
As bathe the newly op'ning flower
That blooms in some ambrosial bower,
'Midst heavenly scenes I seem to rove,
And taste the nectar'd feasts of Jove.

If thus, my Fulvia, you can fire,
And melt my soul with warm desire,
And bid me prove in every kiss
The summit of celestial bliss,
Why then deny with cruel charms
To crown at once my longing arms,

And when my soul in joy would live
Embitter ev'ry sweet you give?
Is 't that you fear lest in that hour
My soul imbibe celestial pow'r,
And from your fond embrace I rise
A god, and seek my native skies,
And all that once delighted shun
To roam Elysium's bowers alone?

My more than life, my only care,
Oh! cease that vain, that foolish fear;
Where'er those beaming eyes of thine
With soul-entrancing lustre shine,
There too shall my Elysium be,
And that be more than heav'n to me.

X.

BAIF.

Come hither, and give me moist kisses,
    Dear girl, such as none ever gave!
What, wouldst thou then number my blisses,
    And ask me how many I'll have?

As well might you have me tell over
   The waves when in ocean they roar,
Or the shells that lie scatter'd, and cover
   The sands on the surge-beaten shore;

Or the bees that on Hybla are winging
   From blossom to blossom their flight;
Or the shouts of the mob, when their ringing
   Applause greets their emperor's sight.

I know not the number of kisses
   That Lesbia was ask'd for, or gave
But sure, who can number his blisses
   Can never have many to crave.

———

XI.

MURET.

When my fond lips would snatch the kiss
   My eyes with envy view the bliss,
And fear to lose those charms on which they dwell
   And, oh! whene'er I strive to raise
   My eyes to you, and fondly gaze,
At once my lips the vain attempt repel.

Such are the charms your lips display,
   So tempt me with their rosy hue,
As steal the magnet's force, so they
   At once attract my lips to you.
Thus, beauteous tyrant, you control,
Thus steal me from myself, and sway my am'rous
   soul.

XII.

SAVAGE.

Happy the man who in thy sparkling eyes
   His am'rous wishes sees reflecting play;
Sees little laughing Cupids glancing rise,
   And in soft swimming languor die away.

Still happier he to whom thy meanings roll,
   In sounds that love, harmonious love inspire
On his charm'd ear sits rapt his list'ning soul,
   Till admiration form intense desire.

Half deity is he who warm may press
   Thy lip soft swelling to the kindling kiss;
And n av that lip assentive warmth express,
   Till love draw willing love to ardent bliss

Circling thy waist, and circled in thine arms,
  Who, melting on thy mutual melting breast,
Entranc'd enjoys love's whole luxurious charms
  Is all a god!—is all of heav'n possess'd!

———

XIII.

T. MOORE.

SWEETLY you kiss, my Lais, dear!
But, while you kiss, I feel a tear
Bitter, as those when lovers part
In mystery, from your eye-lid start;
Sadly you lean your head to mine,
And round my neck in silence twine,
Your hair along my bosom spread,
All humid with the tears you shed!
Have I not kiss'd those lids of snow?
Yet still, my love, like founts they flow,
Bathing our cheeks, whene'er they meet—
Why is it thus? do tell me, sweet!
Ah! Lais, are my bodings right?
Am I to lose you? is to-night
Our last——go, false to heav'n and me,
Your very tears are treachery.

XIV.

PONTANUS.

WHEN thy clos'd lips the joyless kiss impart,
Nor thy warm breath comes glowing from thy
    heart,
A something saddens all my soul, I feel
E'en on my lips the silent kiss grow chill;
But when thy swelling lips reply to mine,
And my warm spirit flies to mix with thine,
My pulses fail, sense, strength, and colour fly,
And pale, and breathless in thine arms I lie.
Come, kiss me close, and with each glowing kiss
O let our spirits mingle into bliss!
But leave no space through which my soul can fly,
Lest in thy circling arms thy lover die.

XV.

PLATO.

WHENE'ER thy nectar'd kiss I sip,
   And drink thy breath, in melting twine,
My soul then flutters to my lip,
   Ready to fly and mix with thine.

XVI.

T. MOORE.

The kiss that she left on my lip,
  Like a dew-drop shall lingering lie,
'Twas nectar she gave me to sip,
  'Twas nectar I drank in her sigh.

The dew that distill'd in that kiss,
  To my soul was voluptuous wine;
Ever since it is drunk with the bliss,
  And feels a delirium divine.

———

XVII.

[From the Italian.]

The bee sips honey in each flow'ret's bell,
Thence bearing tempers in her waxen cell;
Whence man prepares the rich Metheglins juice,
And gods their sweet nectareous draughts produce.
But on thy lips hang sweeter dews, my fair,
Bees seek in flowers, but I find honey there;
There Venus spreads ambrosia to my taste,
And she alone can yield the sweet repast.

XVIII.

SANNAZAR.

Oh! give, when I ask thee, as many sweet kisses
  As fair Lesbia gave to her poet of yore,
Till not e'en the stars shall out-number our
    blisses,
    Or sands that are spread on the surge-beaten
    shore.

Let their sums be as countless as leaves that are
    playing
    On the forest's green boughs when the summer
    is near,
Or the hues of the field when, with flow'rets
    arraying
    Its bosom, spring breathes her warm gales on
    the year:

Or the fishes that swim in the ocean's deep bosom,
    Or pinions that beat the wide vault in their
    flight;
Or the bees that, still roving from blossom to
    blossom,
    Collect their sweet treasures by morn's early
    light.

L

If these, my dear maid, by thy bounty be given,
  As countless, and sweet as thy lover demands,
For them would he spurn all the raptures of
    heaven,
  And the nectar that sparkles in Ganymede's
    hands.

———

XIX.

GUARINI.

Ah! canst thou, cruel nymph, suppose
  One kiss rewards thy am'rous youth?
Enough rewards his tender woes,
  His long, long constancy and truth?

Think not thy promis'd kindness paid
  By simple kissing;—for the kiss
Is but an earnest, beauteous maid,
  Of more substantial future bliss.

Sweet kisses only were design'd
  Our warmer raptures to improve;
Kisses were meant soft vows to bind
  The honied seals of mutual love.

XX.

RANDOLPH.

ARE kisses all?—they but forerun
Another duty to be done:
What would you of that minstrel say,
Who tunes his pipe, and will not play?
Say, what are blossoms in their prime,
That ripen not in harvest time?
Or what are buds that ne'er disclose
The long'd-for sweetness of the rose;
So kisses to a lover's guest
Are invitations, not the feast.

———

XXI.

COME, press my lips, and I will press
  Those humid lips to mine,
And with these wreathing arms caress
  That Laïs form of thine.

Around that rich expansive scene.
  Which all my soul inspires,
I'll twine my arms, and bask between
  Those hills till love expires.

L 2

O! who would wish to cling to life
  If woman were not in it?
O! who would bear its endless strife,
  Without her smile, a minute?

Give but to me her sunny smile,
  Her liquid, balmy kiss;
And though in torment all the while,
  To me it would be bliss.

But without her, all dull and drear
  Are Pleasure's sweetest bowers;
And without her the groves are sear,
  And drooping all the flowers.

She gives to Nature's widest range
  Its most prolific heat;
And without her, the scene would change,
  And heaven be incomplete.

But then of all the darling race,
  There's none I love like thee;
For thou hast got the prettiest face,
  The warmest heart for me.

And when we meet, it seems as though
  There's none could love so well,
Whose hearts could feel so warm a glow,
  Or with such rapture swell.

For in the maze of bliss we taste
  Of every dear delight,
And, planning schemes of rapture, waste
  The long and feverish night,

Till both exhausted—both undone—
  We turn aside and say:
" How swift the midnight hours have run
  To meet the morning ray."

But ere the morning ray appear,
  We'll turn to love again;
And every kiss shall be sincere,
  And not a kiss in vain.

———

XXII.

BEN JONSON.

For love's sake kiss me once again,
I long, and should not beg in vain,
  There's none to spy or see;
    Why do you doubt or stay
I'll taste as lightly as the bee,
That doth but touch his flower, and fly away;

Once more, and, faith, I will be gone:
Can he that loves take less than one?
   Nay, you may err in this,
     And all your bounty wrong:
   This could be call'd but half a kiss:
What we 're to do but once, we should do long.

   I will but mend the last, and tell
   Where now it would have relish'd well;
     Join lip to lip, and try
      Each suck other's breath;
   And whilst our tongues perplexed lie,
Let who will think us dead, or wish our death.

XXIII.

WHEN beauteous Lesbia fires my melting soul,
(She who the torch and bow from Cupid stole,)
By many a smile, by many an ardent kiss,
And with her teeth imprints the tell-tale bliss,
Thro' all my frame the madd'ning transport
    glows,
Thro' every vein the tide of rapture flows.
As many stars as o'er heaven's concave shine,
Or clusters as adorn the fruitful vine,

So many blandishments, voluptuous joys,
T' inflame my breast the wily maid employs.
But dearest Lesbia, gentle mistress, say,
Why thus d'ye wound my lips in am'rous play?
With kisses, smiles, and ev'ry wanton art,
Why raise the burning fever of my heart?
Let us, my love, on yon soft couch reclin'd,
Each other's arms around each other twin'd,
Yield to th' pleasing force of strong desire,
And, panting, struggling, both at once expire.
For, O my Lesbia! sure that death is sweet
Which lovers in the fond contention meet.

———

XXIV.

GUARINI.

WHEN o'er the virgin check we meet
   Health's tender-blooming roses spread,
To kiss those roses may be sweet,
   To kiss them on their native bed.

Full well experience'd lovers know,
   And chief the few who blissful burn,
That kiss is lifeless we bestow
   On charms that yield no kind return.

But sure those kisses breathe delight,
　　Where love the sweetly-vengeful dart,
Exchanges, while fond lips unite,
　　Lips echoing soft as kisses part.

When one warm wish inflames the pair,
　　Not less endearing kisses prove;
Each gives, each takes, an equal share,
　　Sweet interchange of sweetest love.

Kiss the dear lip, the swelling breast,
　　The snow-white hand, the forehead kiss!
'T is by the lip the joy's express'd,
　　'Tis the kind lip repays the bliss.

When lovers' lips in transport join,
　　Their souls to share that transport fly,
And, as their mingling breaths combine,
　　The purple gems with life supply.

Then each inspired kiss imparts,
　　In sounds half-utter'd, half-suppress'd,
The tender secrets of their hearts,
　　Secrets to lips alone confess'd.

Where soul is thus with soul entwin'd,
　　The living rapture is improv'd;
'T is rapture of the sweetest kind,
　　To kiss when kiss'd, to love when lov'd.

XXV.

THERE is a sweet, a pleasing death,
A soft suspension of the breath,
　Replete with tend'rest bliss:
I find it in my Lucy's arms,
I taste it in her ripen'd charms,
　And in her murm'ring kiss.

Wild fancy riots in the thonght
Of rapture with endearment fraught,
　What mortal sense like this?
For you to catch my flecting breath,
To share in that delicious death
　Which hovers on your kiss.

———

XXVI.

INTENT to frame some new design of bliss,
The wanton Cyprian queen compos'd a kiss:
An ample portion of ambrosial juice
With mystic skill she temper'd first for use.
This done, her infant work was well benew o
With choicest nectar; and o er all she strew'd

Part of the honey which sly Cupid stole,
Much to his cost, and blended with the whole;
Then that soft scent which from the violet flows,
She mix'd with spoils of many a vernal rose;
Each gentle blandishment in love we find,
Each graceful winning gesture, next she join'd:
And all those joys that in her zone abound,
Made up the kiss, and the rich labour crown'd.
Consid'ring now what beauteous nymph might
    prove
Worthy the gift, and worthy of her love,
She fix'd on Chloe as her fav'rite maid,
To whom the goddess, sweetly smiling said:
" Take this, my fair, to perfect ev'ry grace,
And on thy lips the fragrant blessing place."

XXVII.

Come, let me touch those pouting lips,
From whence the roving zephyr sips
    Love's most delicious spirit;
Throw round that snowy neck my arms,
Encompass all those lovely charms,
    And all thy soul inherit.

The rose that blooms on yonder tree,
Sweet woman, much resembles thee
  In elegance and nature·
It lives to-day in beauty's bloom,
But, ere to-morrow's sun, the tomb
  May shroud its every feature.

Then let us pluck the charming flow'r,
And share its sweets the fleeting hour
  Indulgent heaven bestoweth;
'Tis folly, love, to pass it by,
'Twere wisdom too for you and I
  To tear it whence it groweth.

Then since in this we both agree,
I turn the moral, love, on thee,
  And ask why thus we trifle?
The rose may bloom another day,
And death may snatch the flow'r away,
  And all its beauty rifle.

Then since it is so frail a flow'r,
The victim of a day an hour,
  O! let us now enjoy it;
For e'er to-morrow's sun go down,
Indignant heaven may sternly frown,
  And secretly destroy it.

XXVIII.

DRUMMOND.

THOUGH I with strange desire
To kiss those rosy lips am set on fire,
    Yet will I cease to crave
      Sweet kisses in such store,
      As he who long before
In thousands them from Lesbia did receive
    Sweetheart, but once me kiss,
      And I by that sweet bliss
E'en swear to cease you to importune more;
    Poor one no number is;
Another word of me you shall not hear
After one kiss, but still one kiss, my dear!

XXIX.

[From the French.]

GIVE me one gentle kiss, I cried:
  And Anne, to stay my fleeting breath,
Scarce touching, to my lips applied
  Her own, and snatch'd me from the gates of
    death.

Ah! why with so short-liv'd a boon,
  My fleeting soul to earth restore?
Why give and take it back so soon?
  Death from thy lips, dear maid, would please me
    more.

———

XXX.

LOVELY Lydia, lovely maid!
Either rose in face's display'd,
Roses of a blushing red
O'er thy lips and cheeks are shed;
Roses of a paly hue
In thy fairer charms we view.
Now thy braided hair unbind;
Now, luxuriant, onconfin'd,
Let thy wavy tresses flow—
Tresses bright of burnish'd glow.

Bare thy iv'ry neck, my fair;
Now thy snowy shoulders bare:
Bid the vivid lustre rise
In thy passion-streaming eyes.
See, the lucent meteors gleam
See, they peak the watchful flame

And how gracefully above,
Modell'd from the bow of love,
Are thy arching brows display'd
Soft'ning in a sable shade ;
Let a warmer crimson streak
The velvet of thy downy cheek:
Let thy l'ps, that breathe perfume,
Deeper purple now assume :
Give me little billing kisses,
Intermix'd with murm'ring blisses.
Soft, my love,—my a gel, stay,
Soft,—you suck my breath away ;
Drink the life-drops of my heart,
Draw my soul from every part:
Scarce my senses can sustain
So much pleasure, so much pain ;
Hide thy broad voluptuous breast,
Hide thy balmy heav'n of rest.
See, to feast th' enamour'd eyes,
How the snowy hillocks rise,
Parted by the luscious vale
Whence luxuriant sweets exhale ;
Nature fram'd thee but t' inspire
Never-ending fond desire.

Again, above its envious vest,
See, thy bosom heaves confess'd ;

Hide the rapt'rous dear delight,
Hide it from my ravish'd sight;
Hide it,—for through all my soul
Tides of madd'ning transport roll:
Venting now th' impassion'd sigh,
See me languish, see me die!
Tear not from me then thy charms,
Snatch, oh! snatch me to thy arms;
With a life-inspiring kiss
Wake my sinking soul to bliss.

———

XXXI.

MARINI.

Yes, beauteous Queen;—thy son, they say,
Thy wanton son is gone astray:
Nay, Venus, more;—'t is said, from thee
A kiss the sweet reward shall be
To any swain who truly tells
With whom the little wand'rer dwells.
Then grieve no more, nor drop a tear,
For know the little urchin's here;
He, from the search of vulgar eyes,
Conceal'd within my bosom lies:
Now, goddess, as I've told thee this,
Give me, oh give, the promis'd kiss!

XXXII.

BONNEFONS.

CLASP'D, sweet maid, in thy embrace,
While I view thy smiling face,
And the sweets with rapture sip,
Flowing from thy honied lip;
Then I taste in heav'nly state
All that's happy, all that's great:

But, when you forsake my arms,
And displeasure clouds thy charms,
Sudden I, who prov'd so late
All that's happy, all that's great,
Prove the tortures of a ghost
Wand'ring on the Stygian coast.

———

XXXIII.

OH! Rosa, I have never felt
Till now the bliss of wooing,
Or known how soon the soul could melt
With rapture, love, and pain.

But you, bewitching girl! have taught
　My soul to woo sincerely,
And you have robb'd that soul of aught
　It yet had valued dearly.

The kiss you gave the other night,
　Though full of woe and anguish,
Was one for whose intense delight
　My soul in pain could languish.

And keener as the torment grew,
　That kiss would sure be sweeter
And faster as my reason flew,
　Its throbbing joy completer.

Until confounded with the bliss,
　We turn'd awhile to sorrow,
Resolv'd to taste another kiss
　Of equal warmth to-morrow.

Oh! not to-morrow, but to-night
　Let us again indulge it;
And by yon moon's auspicious light,
　I swear not to divulge it.

And if, like yonder moon, my fair
　Grow larger, lovelier, brighter,
With many a warmer kiss I swear
　In future to delight her.

M

XXXIV.

As late upon a bed of flow'rs
I laugh'd away the laughing hours,
With, oh! a more delicious maid
Than frolic fancy e'er display'd;
Wh'le twining roses met our view,
As if to show what we should do;
And gentle zephyrs murmur'd by,
As if to teach us how to sigh:
Methought for many an artful wile,
For sweet the maiden seem'd to smile,
That I might so inflame that breast,
Just peeping o'er her sparkling vest,
That she would give my muse to sing
The raptures that from beauty spring,
When, lighted by affection's fire,
Young Passion weds with warm Desire.
Nor when I dar'd disclose my suit,
Did truth my fancied hopes refute,
For soon I led the yielding fair,
By gentlest words and tend'rest care,
From granting first a sidelong kiss,
To the more dear delightful bliss,
With which the melting soul's replete,
When lips meet lips in kisses sweet;
But when with all that glowing zeal
That heart can feign or passiou feel,

Assur'd she meant to yield to me
The sweetest bud on beauty's tree,
I press'd the nymph with warmest tone
To prove herself, indeed, my own,
She started from my glowing arms,
Then clasp'd around her snowy charms,
And flew across the flow'ry lawn,
Like fairy sprite on fancy borne :
Still starting back a smiling leer,
Which gall'd more deep than frowns severe ;
And, crying, as she skimm'd the ground,—
" My zone was loosen'd, not unbound :
And thanks be to your kind endeavour, .
It now is more secure than ever."

XXXV.

BEAUMONT AND FLETCHER.

Take, ah! take those lips away,
   That so sweetly were forsworn,
And those eyes, the break of day,
   Lights that do mislead the morn :
But my kisses bring again,
Seals of love, but seal'd in vain.

M 3

Hide, oh! hide those hills of snow,
  Which thy frozen bosom bears;
On whose tops the pinks that grow
  Are of those which April wears:
But my poor heart, oh! first set free,
Bound in those icy chains by thee.

———

XXXVI.

PETER PINDAR.

LADIES, I should be sorely griev'd indeed,
Could I once write what you would blush to read,
  But that same poet 'clep'd Jean Fontaine,
Was verily the taste and admiration
Of all the ladies of the Gallic nation,
  Quoted and toasted o'er and o'er again.

Our poet Pope against a naughty word
  Protested—seeming too to shut his door;
Pronouncing all obscenity absurd—
  That ribaldry was folly—nothing more;
Yet Master Pope, who decency so flatters,
Plump'd boldly into certain wicked matters.

Miss Heloise, that warm young lass I ween,
   Says things that cover modesty with shame
I must confes I never saw nineteen
   Pour such an Ætna forth of am'ro is flame.
Since then the lightnings of the ladies' eyes
   Knock not the memories of such poets down,
It striketh me indeed with huge surprise,
   That Peter's purer line should feel a frown.

E'en age delighteth in an am'rous tale;
Love warms his inside like a pot of ale,
   Thaws his cold heart, and makes it beat so
      cheery:
His eyes, that owl-like wink'd upon the day,
Burst open with a keen and twinkling ray,
   And, lo' he hugs and kisses his old deary!

XXXVII.

Give me, Lydia, kisses sweet,
Kisses, Love's delicious treat;
Honied kisses from thy lip,
Cupid's self might joy to sip,
Sweeter than the flow'rs which bloom,
And around shed rich perfume—

Softer than the zephyr's breath
Wafted o'er the flow'ry heath!

   Freely give thy soul to joy;
Mercenary pleasures cloy,
While the voluntary bliss,
Kiss so sweetly answering kiss,
Fills the soul with real pleasure,
Bless'd and blessing without measure.

   Mind not what dull pedants say,
Pleasure beckons, let's away!
Age will guard the am'rous flame,
Then, like them, shall we be tame;
But while nature gives the pow'r,
Let's gaily pass the fleeting hour.

———

XXXVIII.

O! JANNIE, let me freely taste
   Those kisses warm and sweet,
For which, my love, I'd gladly waste
   Whole ages at your feet.

Around that little form of thine,
　O, Jannie, let me throw
These warm luxuriant arms of mine,—
　The warmest thou canst know.

One touch of those impressive arms
　Will please my Jannie more
Than all the wiles, and all the charms,
　Of those she knew before.

For I have heard the girls declare,
　When on their necks reclining,
The warmth that they experienc'd there,
　Was rapture past defining.

But 't is not, Love, for me to tell,
　The pleasures that are past,
Jannie herself may judge as well
　As those who prais'd the last.

But this one bargain, Love, I'll make,
　That if I do not please you,
I'll cease, you little rosy rake,
　For ever more to tease you.

XXXIX.

AARON HILL.

'Twas one May morning, when the clouds un
    drawn
Expos'd, in naked charms, the waking dawn;
When night-fall'n dews, by day's warm courtship
    won,
From reeking roses climb'd to kiss the sun·
Nature, new blossom'd, shed her odours round;
The dewy primrose kiss'd the breeze-swept
    ground;
The watchful cock had thrice proclaim'd the day,
And glimm'ring sunbeams faintly forc'd their way:
When join'd in hand and heart, to church we went,
Mutual in vows, and pris'ners by consent:
Aurelia's heart beat high with mix'd alarms,
But trembling beauty glow'd with double charms,
In her soft breast a modest struggle rose,
How she should seem to like the lot she'd chose;
A smile she thought would dress her looks too gay,
A frown might seem too sad, and blast the day.
But while nor this nor that her will could bow,
She walk'd, and look'd, and charm'd, she knew
    not how.
Our hands, at length, th' unchanging fat bound,
And our glad souls sprang out to greet the sound,

Joys meeting joys unite, and stronger shine,
For passion, purified, grows half divine.
Aurelia, thou art mine! I cried; and she
Sigh'd soft—Now, Damon thou art lord of me!
But what thou, whisper'd she, the knot now tied,
Which only death's keen weapon can divide,
Wilt thou, still mindful of thy raptures past,
Permit the summer of love's hope to last?
Shall not cold wintry frosts come on too soon?
Ah, say! what means the world by honey-moon?
If w so short a space our bliss enjoy,
What toils does love for one poor month employ?
Women thus us'd, like bubbles blown in air,
Owe to their outward charms a sun-gilt glare:
Like them, we glitter to the distant eye,
But grasp'd like them, we do but weep and die.
Let me no more, said I, thou should'st profane the tie,
I fear thy dang'rous eyes with this close kiss,
Nor rouse the heav'n of marriage hopes blaspheme,
But cease from me to speak on this lov'd theme.
There have been wedlock joys of swift decay,
Like lightning, seen at once, and shot away;
But theirs were hopes, which, all unfit to pair,
Like fire and powder, kiss'd, and flash'd to air'
Thy soul and mine, by mutual courtship won,
Meet like two mingling flames, and make but one.
Union of hearts, not hands, does marriage make,
'Tis sympathy of minds keeps love awake.

Our growing days increase of joy shall know,
And thick-sown comforts leave no room for woe.
Thou, the soft-swelling vine, shall fruitful last,
I, the strong elm, will prop thy beauty fast;
Thou shalt strew sweets to soften life's rough way;
And, when hot passions my proud wishes sway,
Thou, like some breeze, shalt in my bosom play.
Thou, for protection, shalt on me depend.
I find in thee a soft and faithful friend;
I, in Aurelia, shall for ever view
At once my care, my fear, my comfort, too;
Thou shalt first partner in my pleasures be,
But all my pains shall, last, be known to thee.
Aurelia heard, and view'd me with a smile,
Which seem'd at once to cherish and revile;
O god of love! she cried, what joys are thine,
If all life's race were wedding-days like mine.

XL.

G. A. STEPHENS.

Ye delicate lovelies, with leave I maintain,
  That happiness here you may find;
To yourselves I appeal for felicity's reign,
  When you meet with a man to your mind.

When gratitude friendship to fondness unites,
   Inexpressive endearments arise;
Then hopes, fears, and fancies, strange doubts
     and delights,
   Are announc'd by those tell-tales the eyes.

Those technical terms in the science of love,
   Cold school men attempt to describe;
But how should they paint what they never can
     prove;
   For tenderness knows not their tribe.

Of all the abuse on enjoyment that's thrown,
   The treatment love takes not amiss
Is the rant of the coxcomb, the sot, and the
     clown,
   Who pretend to indulge on a kiss.

The love of a fribble at self only aims :—
   For sots and clowns—class them with beasts;
No fibre, no atom, have they in their frames,
   To relish such delicate feasts.

In circling embraces, when lips to lips move,
   Description, oh! teach me to praise
The overture kiss to the op'ra of love —
   But beauty would laugh at the phrase.

Love's preludes are kisses, and, after the glay,
  They fill up the pause of delight·
The rich repetitions, which never decay,
  The lips' silent language at night.

The raptures of kissing we only can taste
  When sympathies equal inspire:
And while to enjoyment unbounded we haste,
  Their breath blows the coals of desire.

Again, and again, and again, beauty sips;
  When feeling these pressures excite:
When fleeting life's stopp'd by a kiss of the lips,
  Then sinks in a flood of delight.

———

XLI.

PRESS on my lips, oh! gently press
  Another of those kisses sweet;
And I will fondly dream the rest,
  Till we again in rapture meet.

How long the sad suspense will seem—
  How slowly will the moments fly,
Until in that amorosial dream
  On yonder rosy couch we lie.

Yet, Jannie, I will think I seal
  My vows upon that bosom bare,
And I will think we soon shall feel
  The pleasures we have tasted there.

That bosom, oh! whene'er I dwell
  On that expansive scene of charms,
I feel my every pulse rebel—
  I feel my spirit all in arms.

Then let me, Jannie, one night more
  Devote my soul to love and thee;
Jannie will not, I know, deplore
  That little, trivial grant to me.

O! I would rather lie one night
  Beside those hills of glowing snow,
Than live for ages, where the light
  Of rapture never seems to glow.

Yes, Jannie, and I judge of thee,
  My sweetest, by that very rule;
For thou, innocent girl, like me,
  Were tutor'd in a Cyprian school.

But I can feel for Jannie's woes,
  As if she own'd a fairer name;
And, though a fallen girl, she knows
  I strive to hide each blush of shame.

But while I boast a reasoning mind,
   That feeling, dear, shall ne'er decay;
For though the flow'r hath felt the wind,
   It has not swept the stem away.

Nor shall it feel the tempest's pow'r—
   Nor shall it wither—droop—and die,—
But blooming in contentment's bow'r,
   Delight my ever-watchful eye.

————

XLII.

THE transient season let's improve,
That human life allots to love.
Youth soon, my Cynthia, flies away,
And age assumes its frozen sway:
With elegance and neatness dress'd,
Come, then, in beauty's bloom confess'd,
And in my fond embrace be bless'd.

   Faint strugglings but inflame desire,
And serve to fan the lover's fire;
Then yield not all at once your charms,
But with reluctance fill my arms:

My arms' that shall with eager haste
Encircle now your slender waist :
Now round your neck be careless hung,
And now o'er all your frame be flung.
About your limbs my limbs I'll twice,
And lay your glowing cheek to mine ;
Close to my broader manlier chest
I'll press thy firm proud-swelling breast ;
Now rising high, now falling low,
As passion's tide shall ebb or flow,
My murm'ring tongue shall speak my bliss,
Shall court your yielding lips to kiss ;
Each kiss with thousands I'll repay,
And almost suck your breath away.
A thousand more you then shall give,
And then a thousand more receive :
In transport half-dissolv'd we'll lie,
Venting our wishes in a sigh.

    Quick starting from me, now display
Your loose and discompos'd array
Your hair shall o'er your polish'd brow,
In sweetly-wild disorder flow ·
And those long tresses from behind,
You us'd in artful braids to bind,
Shall down your snowy bosom spread,
Redundant, in a soften'd shade·

And from your wishful eyes shall stream
The dewy light of passion's flame;
While now and then a look shall glance,
Your senses lost in am'rous trance,
That fain my rudeness would reprove,
Yet plainly tells how strong you love:
The roses, height'ning on your cheek,
Shall the fierce tide of rapture speak;
And on your lips a warmer glow
The deepen'd ruby then shall show:
Your breast, replete with youthful fire,
Shall heave with tumults of desire;
Shall heave at thoughts of wish'd-for bliss,
Springing as though 't would meet a kiss:
Down on that heav'n I'll sink quite spent,
And lie in tender languishment;
But soon your charms' reviving pow'r
Shall to my frame new life restore:
With love I'll then my pains assuage,
With kisses cool my wanton rage;
Hang o'er thy beauties till I cloy,
Then cease—and then renew my joy!
The bliss I feel be more divine,
Because the source, the spring, of thine.

XLIII.

Come, let's enjoy the passing hour,
(The only one that's in our pow'r,)
Receive and give the balmy kiss,
And let our souls unite in bliss.

'Tis Nature swells the throbbing vein;
Let not her impulse urge in vain:
To Nature all your charms you owe,
Th' iv'ry neck, the roseate glow.

'Tis Nature fires the panting breast,
And bids the sex in love be blest;
She laughs at tyrant Custom's sway,
And pants were Pleasure's cherubs stray

Was it not Nature made you fair?
Say, would you then destroy her care,
Regardless of the high behest,
To multiply—and to be blest?

The world in ev'ry age the same,
Is less profuse of praise than blame:
And shall it blame that sweet embrace
Which gave existence to i's race?

O come then, Anna, rich in charms:—
Sae came, she rush'd into my arms.
Her lips, her form, with passion burn'd—
She gave that bliss which I return'd.

———

XLIV.

Whoe'er is kiss'd beneath my shade,
Widow, wife, or artless maid,
And culls my fruit to search my heart,
And place it next her counterpart,
True shall her ardent wishes at the moment prove,
Foster'd to life, like me, upon the plant I love.

Should they by fate be grafted on
The hazel, crab, or prickly thorn,
Tasteless, or soon degen'rate, wild,
With cares beset, with tears beguil'd,
Partaking of the nature where they hapless grow,
She 'll rue the baleful plant, thy mystic mistletoe.

Ah, no! the oak her wishes bear,
The nymph by tender love led here;
Come, then, in Christmas gambols play,
And dance the midnight hours away;

And join in song the warbling lute,
And gather kisses with my fruit;
Let her fond bosom still with mutual rapture glow,
She'll bless the evergreen, the sacred mistletoe.

———

XLV.

I LOVE the girl whose humid eye
　Is pregnant with illicit pleasure;
The girl that's neither bold nor shy,
　That foots it to a dying measure.

I hate the dull and simpering miss,
　That seems to scorn, yet loves, the action,
But, Chloe, thy impassion'd kiss
　Is full of heavenly satisfaction.

There's something so beyond expression,
　When near thy angel form I languish,
Darts through me, that its strong impression
　Dispels the keenest throes of anguish.

Sweet truant! when the air is calm,
　And all the scene in peace reposes,
We'll drink the midnight's holy balm,
　On couches strown by Love with roses.

N 3

We'll oft, my sweet! together sigh,
　　And think of what we might be doing,
And read with pleasure's wanton eye
　　The volume of our mutual ruin.

Then let us, Chloe, ope the book,
　　And con its most obscure recesses,
And I'll engage by Chloe's look,
　　She'll feel what it so well expresses.

The task, I own, may well appear
　　More difficult than we discern it;
But, Chloe, if we're both sincere,
　　I'll warrant that we quickly learn it.

———

XLVI.

WHAT souls about to leave their bodies bare,
Forc'd to forsake their long-lov'd mansion there,
The dying anguish, the convulsive pain,
And all the racking tortures they sustain:
And, most of all, tne doubt, the dreadful fear,
When thrust out hence, to go they know not
　　　　where:

My soul such pangs, such sad distraction, knew,
Forc'd by despairing love to part with you.
Fix'd on that face where I could ever dwell,
I sigh'd and shook, and could not say farewell.
Down my sad cheeks did tears in torrents roll,
And death's cold damp sat heavy on my soul,
My trembling eyes swam in a native flood,
As fast as they wept tears, my heart wept blood;
My sinking feet seem'd rooted to their place,
And scarce could bear me to the last embrace.
Gods! where was then my soul? that parting kiss
Was both the last and dearest tale of bliss.
Ah! since that fatal time, I could not boast
Of love, of life, or soul: all, all, is lost.
When the last moment that I had to stay
Call'd me, like one condemn'd to death, away,
Yet oft I turn'd, to take another view,
Oft gaz'd, and sigh'd, and murmur'd out, Adieu!

XLVII.

I watch'd her many a dreary night,
  When death seem'd hovering near,
And saw full many a dear delight
  In every glance appear.

She look'd as if she dar'd not love,
  Or fondly question'd mine,
Yet often seem'd intent to prove
  A passion most divine.

She press'd me to her quivering lips,
  And bade me not depart,
And with those eyes that suns eclipse
  Seduc'd my falt'ring heart.

————

XLVIII.

Were it not better, pretty Ruth,
Instead of telling beads, forsooth,
  To number burning kisses?
And 'stead of kneeling at yon shrine,
To have me fondly own thee mine,
  And pay my vows with blisses?

Indeed it will be better sport
To sweetly mix in pleasure's court,
  And yield to her emotions:
And whatsoever now you feel,
Trust me you'll grow with greater zeal,
  Engag'd in such devotions.

XLIX.

TO A LADY WHO KISSED HER SPARROWS.

Why, Anna, why let sparrows sip
The nectar from your rosy lip?
Ask but your heart—it will suggest
They value not what makes me blest.

———

L.

TO THE SPARROWS WHICH WERE KISSED.

Ye sparrows, who from Anna's lip,
Divinest nectar hourly sip,
   Nor yet of pleasure die,
How adverse is the will of Fate!
You for her kisses to create,
   To pine without them I!

To you unconscious of the bliss
The soul inhales from Anna's kiss,
   The boon divine is given;
Whilst I am doom'd to know its charm,
Yet be denied the fragrant balm
   Bedewing that rich heaven.

LI.

As am'rous prelate, legends say,
Near Chloe, blooming, young, and gay,
Soon felt the force of passion rise;
Its fire was caught from Chloe's eyes:
His holy hand o'er treasures rov'd—
Gems which might a saint have mov'd:
" What are you doing, sir?" she cried,
And as he kiss'd her, gently sigh'd:
" Doing, sweet nun!—*in partibus*
I'm visiting my diocese!"

LII.

MARTIAL.

Come, Chloe, and give me sweet kisses,
  For sweeter sure girl never gave;
But why, in the midst of my blisses,
  Do you ask me how many I'd have?
I'm not to be stinted in pleasure,
  Then prithee, my charmer, be kind:
For whilst I love you above measure,
  To numbers I'll ne'er be confin'd.

Count the bees that on Hybla are playing,
  Count the flow'rs that enamel the fields;
Count the flocks that on Tempe are straying,
  Or the grain that rich Sicily yields:
Go number the stars in the heav'n,
  Count how many sands on the shore;
When so many kisses you've giv'n,
  I still shall be craving for more.

To a heart full of love let me hold thee,
  To a heart which, dear Chloe, is thine:
With my arms I'll for ever enfold thee,
  And twist round thy limbs like a vine.
What joy can be greater than this is
  My life on thy lips shall be spent;
But the wretch that can number his kisses,
  With few will be ever content.

LIII.

If love be perdition, why Laura and I
  Are meant for the lowest abyss;
For what with the magic that lurks in her eye,
  And the sweetness and warmth of her kiss

I ne'er have forgotten the lesson she taught me,
    When toying together we lay,
Till swooning in transport she tenderly caught me,
    And stole all my senses away.

But who would desire a heaven more bright
    Than that which her neck can impart?
Let that treasure be mine, and a world of delight,
    Though in torment, would gladden my heart.

Kiss, Laura! again; and again let me press
    That bosom far whiter than snow;
For since we are doom'd to the realms of distress
    Down the river of pleasure we'll go.

LIV.

HORACE.

'Twas night, and heav'n, intent with all its eyes,
    Gaz'd on the dear deceitful maid:
    A thousand pretty things she said,
    A thousand kisses sweetly paid,
From me, deluded me, her falsehood to disguise.

She clasp'd me in her soft encircling arms,
    She press'd her glowing lips to mine,—
    The clinging ivy, or the curling vine,
    Did ne'er yet so closely twine:
Who could be man and bear the lustre of her
    charms?

And thus she swore: " By all the powers above,
    When winter storms shall cease to roar,
    When summer seas shall rise no more,
    When waves their bounding cease,
Neæra then, and not till then, shall cease to love."

Ah! false Neæra! perjured fair!—but know
    I have a soul too great to bear
    A rival's proud insulting air;
    Another may be found as fair,
As fair, ungrateful nymph! and far more just than
    thou.

Shouldst thou repent, and at my feet be laid,
    Dejected, penitent forlorn,
    And all thy former follies mourn,
    Thy proffer'd passion I would scorn·
The gods shall do me right on that devoted head·

KISSES

LV.

Cease your music, gentle swains;
Saw ye Delia cross the plains?
Every thicket, every grove,
Have I rang'd to find my love:
A kid, a lamb, my flock, I'll give,
Tell me only, doth she live?

White her skin as mountain snow
In her cheek the roses blow;
And her eye is brighter far
Than the beaming morning star,
When her ruddy lips ye view,
'Tis a berry moist with dew:
Kisses sweet those lips impart,
Rapture giving to the heart.
Her breath, oh! it is a gale
Passing o'er a fragrant vale,
Passing, when a friendly show'r
Freshens every herb and flow'r,
Wide her bosom opens, gay
As the primrose dell in May;
Sweet as violet-borders growing
Over fountains ever flowing.
Like the tendrils of the vine
Do her auburn tresses twine;

Glossy ringlets all behind,
Streaming buxom to the wind;
When along the lawn she bounds,
Light as wind before the hounds;
And the youthful ring she fires,
Hopeless in their fond desires,
As her little feet advance,
Wanton in the winding dance.

Tell me, shepherds, have you seen
My delight, my love, my queen?

LVI.

GALLUS.

My goddess Lydia, heav'nly fair,
As lilies sweet, as soft as air,
Let loose thy tresses, spread thy charms,
And to my love give fresh alarms.

Oh! let me gaze on those bright eyes,
Though sacred lightning from them flies;
Show me that soft, that modest grace,
Which paints with charming red thy face.

Give me ambrosia in a kiss,
That I may rival Jove in bliss;
That I may mix my soul with thine,
And make the pleasure all divine.

Oh! hide thy bosom's killing white,
(The milky-way is not so bright,)
Lest you my ravish'd soul oppress
With beauty's pomp and sweet excess.

Why draw'st thou from the purple flood
Of my kind heart the vital blood?
Thou art all over endless charms—
Oh! take me, dying, to thine arms.

LVII.

FROM Anna's dear lip
Though nectar I sip,
That nectar insipid would prove,
If there were no charms
To find in her arms
Beyond the sweet kiss of her love.

The kiss, it is true,
For children may do,
The passionless, aged, or grave;
But I, in full flow'r,
Feel Nature's great pow'r,
And food more substantial I crave.

I look on a kiss
As the portal of bliss
To him unto whom it is given;
A key that insures
Your way through the doors
Which lead to the Paphian heav'n.

LVIII.

BATH'D in the freshest dew of night,
Roses blush a softer light;
So blush thy lips from many a kiss
Snatch'd in a long, long night of
Blush, and steal a tint more bright
From thy skin of snowy white.
Thus violets shed a purer blue,
Held in some hand of lily hue;

Thus early rip'ning cherries glow,
'Mid blossoms white that later blow,
When summer dress'd in garlands sweet,
And dew-ey'd Spring together meet.

Ah! must I leave thee, while I sip
Thy soul embodied on thy lip;
Then let thy pulpy lip retain
The dewy glow, till night again
Bring me, while others sink to rest,
To wake in raptures on thy breast:
But should these lovely lips of thine
Ere then bless any lips but mine,
Pale may they turn! as deadly pale
As I should turn to know thee frail!

LIX.

BEN JONSON.

For love's sake kiss me once again;
I long, and should not beg in vain—
　Here's none to spy or see;
Why do you doubt or stay?
　I'll taste as lightly as the bee
That doth but touch his flow'r, and flies away.

LX.

THE FAIR CIRCASSIAN AND SOLOMON.

SAPHIRA.

O Love, thy mighty burnings who can bear?
What thirst, what fervor can with mine compare!
With speed conduct me to the lovely swain
That fires my soul, and causes all my pain;
'Tis only that dear youth whose balmy kiss
Can mitigate my smart with healing bliss.
O come, my dearest, come, and hither bring
Thy lips adorn'd with all the blooming spring;
A thousand sweets their fragrant atoms blend,
Which, in a gale of joy, thy breath attend;
Such soothing cordials to my soul apply,
Heal me with kisses, love, or else I die;
With poignant tasteful kisses, such as thine,
Whose flavour far excels the richest wine.
Me and my charmer now, from noontide bow'rs,
To spend in various scenes our blissful hours,
Love the banqueting pavilion brings,
And o'er our heads unfurls his trembling wings.
With fev'rish heat he seizes every part,
Burns in my veins, and revels in my heart.
He sinks to slumbers on the rosy bed,
And on his arms I lean my love-sick head;

o

On his left arm my love-sick head I place,
His right enfolds me with a warm embrace.
Soft, I adjure you, by the nimble fawns
And hinds that bound across the flow'ry lawns,
Ye sportive damsels, that ye softly move,
Nor with your voices wake my sleeping love.
Approach, fond maids, and see my lovely king
Crown'd with the beauties of the gaudy spring,
The garland his indulgent mother wove,
Against the solemn festival of love.

SOLOMON.

How fair art thou, my queen! thy charms how
    bright;
For pleasure form'd, and finish'd for delight:
Tall as the palm thy mien; thy juicy breast,
Like clust'ring grapes, inviting to be press'd.
Let me the straight, the stately pole ascend;
Grasp'd in my arms the blooming boughs shall
    bend;
The clust'ring vine in my embrace shall bleed,
And on the fragrant balmy breath I'll feed.

SAPHIRA.

Thy transports, love, with what delight I hear;
Such fondness ravishes my list'ning ear.
With thee I'll range the distant lonely fields,
Where the fresh spring eternal pleasure yields;

Where the lone village, free from noisy strife,
Unheeded drinks the real sweets of life.
There let us lodge, and with the morning sun
Our course of pleasing toil together run;
Observe the vine its tender bud disclose,
How with young bloom the new pomegranate
    glows;
How rip'ning fruits in embryo appear,
The grateful prospect of a plenteous year.
There, on some bank reclin'd, whilst o'er head
Embow'ring jasmines their sweet odours shed,
Clasping and clasp'd, with ever twining arms,
Uninvied, I'll enjoy thy manly charms,
Give up my hidden beauties to thy sight,
And die in ecstasies of full delight.

LXI.

COURTIER.

Goddess! I do love a girl
Ruby-lip'd and tooth'd with pearl
If so he I may but prove
Lucky in this maid I love,
I will promise there shall be
Myrtles offered up to thee.

LXII.

Bloom of beauty, early flow'r
Of the blissful bridal bow'r;
Thou, thy parents' pride and care,
Fairest offspring of the fair;
Lovely pledge of mutual love,
Angel seeming from above,—
Was it not thou day by day
Dost the very sex betray,
Female more and more appear,
Female, more than angel dear;
How to speak thy face and mien,
(Soon too dangerous to be seen,)
How shall I, or shall the muse,
Language of resemblance choose?
Language like thy mien and face,
Full of sweetness, full of grace?

By the next returning spring,
When again the linnets sing,—
When again the lambkins play,
Pretty sportlings, full of May;
When the meadows next are seen,
Sweet enamel! white and green,
And the year, in fresh attire,
Welcomes every gay desire,

Blooming on shalt thou appear
More inviting than the year;
Fairer sight than orchard snows
Which beside a river blows.

   Yet another spring I see,
And a brighter bloom in thee;
And another round of time,
Circling, still improves thy prime.
And, beneath the vernal skies,
Yet a year or more shall rise,
Ere thy beauties kindly slow,
In each finish'd feature glow;
Ere, in smiles and in disdain,
Thou exert thy maiden reign,
Absolute to save or kill
Fond beholders at thy will.

   Then the taper-moulded waist,
With a span of ribbon brac'd,
And the swell of either breast,
And the wide high-vaulted chest,
And the neck so white and round,
Little neck with brilliants bound,
And the store of charms which shine
Above in lineal eyes d'vi.
Crowded in a narrow spa
To complete the desp'rate face;

These alluring pow'rs, and more,
Shall enamour'd youths adore;
These and more, in courtly lays,
Many an aching heart shall praise.

———

LXIII.

HILL.

O VENUS! awful sov'reign of the spring,
    Could I like thy Lucretius sing,
Here would I pause thy wonders to relate;
    Here would I pause to hymn thy praise
In adamantine words, more strong than fate,
    And everlasting as his lays.

O'er seas and deserts, undismay'd,
    Strengthen'd by thy inspiring breath,
The timorous and the bashful maid,
    Faces both infamy and death.

Driv'n by the incens'd divinity,
    Confounding equity and truth,
Order, and rank, and consanguinity,
    And loathsome age, and blooming youth.

Behold the frantic passion, how it burns,
  Like a wild beast breaks every tie:
Laughs at the priest, the legislator spurns;
  And gives both heav'n and earth the lie!

Let youth and insolence alone,
  Provoke thy vengeance every hour;
But, oh! spare those that know, that own,
  Adore, and tremble, at thy pow'r.

With thy propitious dews descend,
  And hear the tender virgin's sighs,
The humble and the meek defend,
  And bid the prostrate suppliant rise.

LXIV.

Grow to my lip, thou sacred kiss,
On which my soul's beloved swore
That there should come a time of bliss,
When she would mock my hopes no more;
And fancy shall thy glow renew,
In sighs at morn, and dreams at night,
And none shall steal thy balmy dew
Till thou'rt absolv'd by rapture's rite.

Sweet hars that are to make me bless'd
Oh! fly, like breezes, to the goal,
And let my love, my more than soul,
Come panting to this fever'd breast;
And while in every glance I drink
The rich o'erflowings of her mind,
Oh! let her all impassion'd sink,
In sweet abandonment resign'd,
Blushing for all our struggles past,
And murmuring, "I am thine at last."

———

LXV.

PETER PINDAR.

When we dwell on the lips of the lass we adore,
   Not a pleasure in nature is missing:
May his soul be in heav'n, he deserv'd it, I'm
     sure,
   Who was first the inventor of kissing.

Master Adam, I verily think, was the man,
   Whose discovery will ne'er be surpass'd.
Well, since the sweet game with creation began,
   To the end of the world may it last.

LXVI.

The days, the weeks, the months of bliss
  That we, as ose, have pass'd together,
Th' impression of your balmy kiss
  At Ri beautie, in the summer weather,

Shall long remain fix'd in my mind,
  To please me when my spirit's low,
For they still leave a joy behind,
  To soften every sting of woe.

O! I remember well how sweet
  All nature seem'd, when thro' the corn
You tripp'd on th se bewitching feet,
  Beneath the rosy tints of morn.

Bless'd be those feet, so swift so airy,
  Methinks I see them glide along,
Light as the motion of a fairy,
  That trips it to the zephyr's song.

Bless'd be those eyes, whose glances sweet
  Were on eas of her inward worth,
In them my worldly fate I meet,
  My best, my dearest hope on earth.

So modest in her look,—her mien
   So pleasing, airy, light, and easy,
That one might think her Fancy's queen,
   A spirit only form'd to please ye.

O! I can never view the days
   We spent in Richmond's rosy bowers,
Where memory still delighted strays,
   Amidst the morn and evening hours.

Without possessing all those dreams
   Which led my wandering feet astray,
And form'd the world not as it seems,
   Merely to steal my peace away.

LXVII.

T. MOORE.

When infant bliss in roses slept,
Cupid upon his slumber crept,
And while a balmy sigh he stole
Exhaling from the infant's soul,
He smiling said, " With this, with this,
I'll scent my Julia's burning kiss!"

Nay more, he stole to Venus' bed,
Ere yet the sanguine flush had fled,
Which love's tenderest, dearest flame
Had kindled through her panting frame.
Her soul still dwelt on memory's themes,
Still floated in voluptuous dreams,
And ere what joy she felt before
In slumber now was acting o'er.
From her ripe lips, which seem'd to thrill
As in the hour of kisses still,
As amorous to each other clung,
He stole the dew that trembling hung,
And smiling said, " With this, with this,
I'll bathe my Julia's burning kiss!"

LXVIII.

WINDS! whisper gently while she sleeps,
    And fan her with your cooling wings,
While she her crown of beauty keeps
    From time and yet unrifled springs.

Glide over beauty's field her face;
    To kiss her lip and cheek be bold;
But with a calm and stealing pace,
    Neither too rude, nor yet too cold.

Play in her beams, and crisp her hair
   With such a gale as wings soft love;
And with so sweet, so rich an air,
   As breathes from the Arabian grove.

A breath as hush'd as lover's sigh,
   Or that unfolds the morning's door:
Sweet as the winds that gently fly
   To sweep the spring's enamell'd floor.

———

LXIX.

WITH every girl of whom I sing,
For whom I've touch'd the silver string,
   Or morning, noon, or night;
With every one I've kiss'd and toy'd,
And many a silent hour employ'd
   In banquets of delight.

They all appear'd to shun the bliss,
But when they once had felt a kiss,
   They long'd and sigh'd for others;
Until at last, so freakish grown,
The wicked girls began to own,
   They learn'd it of their mothers.

KISSES.

And verily the girls are right,
For still the aged dames delight
  To sport in those excesses;
Then can we wonder they are caught
Indulging, where they never ought,
  Such libertine caresses?

Indeed, my friend, I had not been
So learned, if I had not seen
  These wicked, wild embraces;
But in those dark and nameless courts,
Where Laïs shines thro' all the sports,
  I've recogniz'd their faces.

—

LXX.

Humid seal of soft affection,
  'Tend'rest pledge of future bliss;
Dearest tie of young connexion,
  Love's first snow-drop, Virgin-kiss.

Speaking silence! dumb confession!
  Passion's birth, and infant's play;
Dove-like fondness, chaste concession,
  Glowing dawn of brighter day.

Sorrowing joy! adieu's last action.
  When ling'ring lips no more must join;
What words can ever speak affection
  So thrilling, so sincere as thine.

Thee th' fond youth untaught and simple,
  Nor on the naked breast can find,
Nor within the cheek's small dimple,—
  Sole offspring thou of lips conjoin'd.

Then haste thee to thy dewy mansion;
  With Hebe spend thy laughing day;
Dwell in her rubied lips' expansion,
• Bask in her eye's propitious ray.

———

LXXI.

Our seat with eglantine was spread,
  And as we mark'd the eve decay,
My Laura smil'd, and softly said,
  " Why pass we thus the hours away?"

I wonder'd much what Laura meant,
  For thro' her eyes such magic flew,
As if she were not quite content,
  And wanted something else to do.

I press'd her lips—the fair one seem'd
  As if she fear'd, yet lov'd, the bliss;
The more I press'd, the more she dream'd
  Of rapture from the silent kiss.

I quick resolv'd, the maid, 'tis true,
  And well she comprehended me;
And as the evening tints withdrew,
  I ask'd her if the deed might be?

Thus after many an effort sweet,
  Beneath the summer's sultry weather
I felt her lips give way—to meet
  The kiss we both enjoy'd together.

———

LXXII.

T. MOORE.

Sweet seducer! blandly smiling,
Charming still, and still beguiling;
Oft I swore to love thee never,
Yet I love thee more than ever.

Why that little wanton blushing,
Glancing eye, and bosom flushing?
Flushing warm, and wily glancing,
All is lovely, all entrancing.

Turn away those lips of blisses—
I am poison'd by thy kisses:
Yet, again, ah! turn them to me:
Ruin's sweet when they undo me.

Oh! be less, be less enchanting;
Let some little grace be wanting;
Let my eyes, when I'm expiring,
Gaze awhile, without admiring.

————

LXXIII.

WEARIED with toying, Love had sunk to sleep
Upon a bank of moss, while o'er him sprang,
Spontaneous, a canopy of flow'rs:
Poppies of scarlet dye, whose nodding heads
Upon his eyelids shed their drowsy balm:
And, intertwin'd with these, the paler rose,
Whose scented blossoms, bath'd in lucid dew,
Woo'd the soft breeze to loiter as it pass'd,

And borrow fragrant coolness.   Near him lay
His bow and quiver, fraught with fatal shafts,
Wing'd in hope, bat e pp'd in tears of woe.
While thus he sl pt, his lovely Psyche came,
So lightly treading, that her snowy foot
Brush'd not the dew-drop from the cowslip's bell
Awhile she stood to gaze, her heav'nly face
Breathing ethereal love; then kneeling down
So gently, that her amber-scented breath
Stirr'd not the gossamer, she cull'd a dart,
And on its point impress'd a balmy kiss
Of love and sweetness redolent; then turn'd
The thrilling weapon on her sleeping spouse,
And, innocently the part, lightly press'd
The point upon his bosom: at the touch
The god awoke, and thro' all his veins
The piercing poison course ing; but his love
When a, beheld, he sunk upon her breast,
His filmy pinions quiv'ring with delight.

LXXIV.

I wish I could like zephyr steal
　To wanton in thy maze vest;
Or thou wouldst now thy bosom veil,
　And take me panting to thy breast

I wish I might a rosebud grow,
  That thou wouldst cull me from the bower,
And place me in that breast of snow,
  Where I should bloom a wint'ry flower.

I wish I were the lily's leaf
  To fade upon that bosom warm;
There I should wither, pale and brief,
  The trophy of thy fairer form.

LXXV.

TUBERVILE,

[On making his mistress's lip bleed.]

DISCHARGE the dole, thou subtle seal,
  It stands in little steed
To curse the kiss that causer is
  Thy cherry lip doth bleed.

Thy blood ascends to make amends
  For damage thou hast done;
For by the same I felt a flame
  More scorching than the sun.

Thou reft'st my heart by secret art,
My spirits were quite subdu'd,
My senses fled, and I was dead,
Thy lips were scarce embru'd.

The kiss was thine, the hurt was mine,
My heart felt all the pain;
'Twas it that bled, and look'd so red,
I tell thee once again!

But if you long to wreak your wrong
Upon your friendly foe,
Come kiss again, and put to pain
The man that hurt you so.

———

LXXVI.

FONTANUS.

She smil'd consenting, and her lips impart
To my parch'd lips one dear delicious kiss,
Whose breath that instant to my fainting heart
Recall'd my spirit from the dark abyss;
A humid kiss, rich with ambrosial dews,
And all the spicy sweets Arabia's shrubs diffuse.

P 3

KISSES.

LXXVII.

ANGERIANUS.

A FLOW'RY bank my Celia press'd,
   Where babbling waters play'd,
And by the stream in gentle rest
   Her languid limbs were laid;

It chanc'd a bee, on busy wing,
   Whom instinct taught to stray,
And gather honied sweets in spring,
   Came murm'ring by that way.

Lur'd by the fragrance of her lip
   The insect hover'd round,
But often, as it stoop'd to sip,
   Fell senseless to the ground:

Till feeling the approach of death,
   What new-born flow'r is this?
It feebly ask'd, with dying breath,
   For thus to die is bliss!

Then sank, and died; and little Love
   A turf upon it plac'd,
And of its fate, in verse above,
   A short memorial trac'd:

" Here lies beneath whom Celia's breath,
 Or nonied lips destroy'd;
But none can tell by which he fell,
 By one, or both he died.

LXXVIII.

STANLEY.

WHEN en thy lips my soul I breathe,
 Which there meets thine;
Freed from their fetters by that death
 Our subtle forms combine:
Thus without bonds of sense they move,
And like two cheruoim converse by love.

 Spirits to chains of death confin'd
  Converse by sense;
But ours, that are by flames refin'd,
  With those weak ties dispense:
Let such in words their minds display,
We in a kiss our mutual thoughts convey.

But since my soul from me doth fly,
     To thee retir'd,
Thou canst not both retain, for I
     Must be by one inspir'd;
Then, dearest, either justly mine
Restore, or in exchange let me have thine,

Yet if thou dost return mine own,
     Oh! take't again!
For 'tis this pleasing death alone
     Gives ease unto my pain:
Kill me once more, or I shall find
Thy pity than thy cruelty less kind.

———

LXXIX.

MARULLUS.

WITH bended bow, young Love had ta'en his
     stand,
When sudden awe repress'd his daring hand;
As quick Neæra saw the youth's surprise,
And on him turn'd the whole artill'ry of her eyes:
Swift as the winds the urchin turn'd away,
And fled from her whom he had meant his prey,

But his bright quiver, charg'd with many a wound,
Loos'd from his back, fell rattling to the ground ;
The fair one seiz'd the glitt'ring prize, and o'er
Her shoulders flinging, in proud triumph bore.
Now, while Love roams disarm'd, a feeble foe,
On gods, and men alike she bends his bow,

———

LXXX.

WYAT.

When first mine eyes did view, and mark,
   Thy fair beauty to behold ;
And when my ears listen'd to hark,
   The pleasant words that thou me told ;
I would as then I had been free
From ears to hear, and eyes to see.

And when my lips 'gan first to move,
   Whereby my heart to thee was known ;
And when my tongue did talk of love,
   To thee that hast true love down thrown ;
I would my lips, and tongue also,
Had then been dumb, no deal to go.

And when my hands have handled aught
   That thee hath kept in memory;
And when my feet have gone and sought
   To find and get thee company;
I would each hand a foot had been,
And I each foot a hand had seen.

And when in mind I did consent
   To follow this my fancy's will;
And when my heart did first relent
   To taste such bait my life to spill;
I would my heart had been as thine,
Or else thy heart had been as mine.

———

LXXXI.

DRUMMOND.

DEAR life, when I do touch
   Those coral ports of bliss,
   Which still themselves do kiss,
And sweetly me invite to do as much;

All panting on thy lips
  My heart my life doth leave,
  Nor sense my senses have,
And inward powers do feel a strange eclipse:
  This death so heavenly well
  Doth me so please, that I
Would never longer seek in sense to dwell,
If that e'er thus I only could but die.

———

LXXXII.

FLAMINIUS.

Hast thou seen, after a summer shower,
  How the lily's leaves are sparkling bright;
Or the tears of night on the rose's flower,
  As they shine like pearls in the morning light?

So on her cheeks, when my Rosa weeps,
  Each tear-drop shines like a glitt'ring gem,
While Love beneath in sly ambush peeps,
  And scatters his shafts at me through them.

LXXXIII.

SANNAZAR.

Six hundred kisses from thy lips I sue,
Six hundred kisses, Nina, are my due;
Not such as sisters to their brothers give,
Or parents from their duteous child receive;
But such as some young maid, but newly wed,
Gives the dear partner of her bridal bed,
Or the fond lover of his fair one's lips,
All lost in soft delirious transport, sips.
These—these delight me—these are doubly dear,
When lips to lips in ecstasy adhere ·
Cold is the kiss that senseless beauty gives,
From such my ardent soul no joy receives.
Oh! rather let me, when thou giv'st the bliss,
Grow to thy lip in each delicious kiss,
There in soft accents breathe my tender joys,
And hear thy raptures in responsive sighs;
Mingling our melting tale of mutual love
In tones as soothing as the am'rous dove.

   Sweet are such raptures, sweeter than the dews
That chymist bees in waxen cells diffuse;
Or the rich nectar, that imperial Jove
Quaffs in bright goblets in the realms above.

Yet, when these joys have heighten'd ev'ry grace,
Wouldst thou but clasp me in thy fond embrace,
Kings should not tempt me thence, nor heaps
    untold
Of sparkling jewels, and persuasive gold:
Not Venus self should lure me from thy arms
With all her rosy prevalence of charms:
Nor Hebe, though to tempt me from my truth,
She promise years of never-fading youth.

LXXXIV.

MURET.

A humid kiss with nectar rich imbu'd,
Ambrosial sweet, she gave in playful mood,
Fragrant as dews from thyme, or cassia drawn
By bees that labour at the glimpse of dawn;
Then burst away in wantonness, and flew
To deep'ning shades, and hid her from my view,
But I id in vain; the power of Love forbade,
And lent his torch, and her retreat betray'd.

Again, my beauteous fair, thy form I hold—
Again I clasp—again these arms enfold:

Again—But why with such disorder'd charms,
My rose, why tremble in my circling arms?
Come, let thy lips the toil of search repay
With balmy kisses varied ev'ry way;
Thrice three I claim, and let thy every kiss
Teem with a rich diversity of bliss.

Oh! dost thou feel, as mouth with mouth unites,
Our souls commingle in the dear delights,
Each rising to the lips forsake the heart,
And hover there, and join its better part?
Thus, ever thus, unite thy soul with mine,
So shall no day our future souls disjoin;
And when this transient scene of life is o'er,
United fly, and seek the Stygian shore.

LXXXV.

BONFADIUS.

Ye grots, ye groves, were witness of my bliss,
When from her lips I snatch'd the nectar'd kiss!
The thrilling joy of life, and sense bereft,
And on her humid lips my soul was left.

But when she saw me pale, and breathless laid,
With fond encircling arms the lovely maid
My languid form drew closer to her breast,
And on my li s a sweeter kiss impress'd;
And scarce had I inhal'd the balmy dew
When to my heart my wand'ring spirit flew.
To me now dearer is the vital flame
Since from her lips, her ruby lips, it came.

———

LXXXVI.

BUCHANAN.

With ev'ry kiss those lips, my fair, bestow
Such nectar'd streams, such rich ambrosia flow,
With gods I seem their heav'nly state to share,
With gods I banquet on celestial fare;
And lost in pleasing dreams of ecstasy,
Seem far more bless'd than e'en a god can be.
But, oh! whene'er those balmy kisses flow
With falsehood mix'd, and treach'ry lurks below,
Then instant I, who shar'd the realms of bliss,
Plunge headlong down to hell's profound abyss,
In darker horrors lost, and deeper woe
Than those that suffer in that world below.

LXXXVII.

PASQUIER.

Dear maid, a gentle kiss impart
  Like that, in innocence of heart,
Which some young girl, with fond caresses
On her fair sister's cheek impresses.
For joys like that, so pure, and chaste,
Must ever please, and ever last.
I hate the kiss of wild desire,
All glowing with voluptuous fire;
Like flames that too intensely play,
The pleasure quickly fades away.

———

LXXXVIII.

DR. ARMSTRONG.

    .... Such ills attend
Obscene and bought embraces. Wiser thou,
Find some soft nymph whom tender sympathy
Attracts to thee: while all her captives else,
Aw'd by majestic beauty, mourn aloof
Her charms to thee, by nuptial vows and choice

More sure, devoted.   Sacrifice to her
The precious hours, nor grudge with such a mate
The summer's day to toy, or winter's night.
Now clasp with dying fondness in your arms
Her yielded waist: now on her swelling breast
Recline your cheek: with eager kisses press
Her balmy lips, and drinking from her eyes
Resistless love, the tender flame confess,
Ineffable but by the murm'ring voice
Of genuine joy. . . . .
. . . . Yet not to love alone
Yield languid all your hours.   The self-same
          cates,
Still offer'd, soon the appetite offend;
The most delicious soonest.   Other joys,
Other pursuits, their equal share demand
Of cultivation.   These, with kindly change,
Will cheer your sweetly-varied days; from these,
With quicker sense you shall, and firmer nerve,
Return to love, when love again invites.
Be those the least neglected which inform
With virtue, sense, and elegance, the mind;
Those that before were amiable improve,
And lend to love new grace and dignity.
Life too has serious cares, which, madly scorn'd,
The means of pleasure melt.   And age will come,
When love, alas! the flower of human joys,
Must shrink in horrid frost'

LXXXIX.

SECUNDUS.

Pleasure has bounds; too greedily pursu'd,
  Enjoyment ceases, and disgust ensues;
Thus, at first glance, some recent painting view'd,
  The vernal landscape smiles in all its brightest
      hues;
But stand, and gaze awhile, and by degrees
The eye grows tir'd, the colours cease to p'ease;
Its beauties vanish, and its faults arise,
You think of other times, and criticise.

THE END.

www.ingramcontent.com/pod-product-compliance
Lightning Source LLC
Chambersburg PA
CBHW020104030726
47498CB00006B/1947